Bethune

The Only Person
Alive
In the World

a novel
by
John Passfield

Rock's Mills Press
Oakville, Ontario

Published by
ROCK'S MILLS PRESS
www.rocksmillspress.com

For information, including Library and Archives Canada Cataloguing in Publication data, please contact us at customer.service@rocksmillspress.com.

Cover illustration: A self-portrait by Norman Bethune, 1935.

Cover design: Craig Passfield

Author's website: www.johnpassfield.ca

ISBN-13: 978-1-77244-093-5 (paperback)

Chapter 1

Canada 1

Setting up a new practice. Stratford, Ingersoll, Aylmer, Detroit. Changing cities from time to time as the spirit moves. Setting my glass of wine down on my desk as I stand up on a chair and hammer a nail. Adjusting my diploma on my office wall. Cranking up the Victrola. Two or three of our favourite songs. Frances and I whirling around the desk. Vernon and Irene Castle. The élan of a fancy-dress ball. The patients will pour in through the front door! The secretary will take their names! You have an appointment, I presume? You have your cheque-book with you? The doctor is busy with a patient, but will be with you soon! The bustling nurse, the shelves of pills, the table with instruments sterilized, many of which the doctor has invented himself! A pause for a sip of wine. Then up on the chair to straighten the crooked diploma. The Victrola chuckles and chortles. Frances and I in love, whirling around the room at a fancy-dress ball.

I am the only person.

A girl with ruddy cheeks and an apple complexion.
A man painting a mural inside a cage.
A physician riding along in a jaunty roadster.

I am the only person alive.

A sick daughter sweating feverishly in the tent. Hunter-gatherers search-ing in a meadow. An elderly woman finds the precious herb.

I am the only person alive in the world.

Why is the pressure of thought so enormous?
At what depth, underwater, does the skull implode?
At what temperature, in the furnace, do the brains boil?

To build a practice which will make me the envy of every doctor in my profession. To be able to enjoy the finest wines and hang the best paintings on my walls. To have Frances and I take romantic trips to Paris. To travel to Swit-zerland in the winter and to stay in a fancy chalet. To spend the whole day skiing down the powdery slopes of the Alps. A blazing fireplace and a glass of the finest champagne. The firelight as it sparkles in Frances's eyes. To be known as an innovator. To sweep the stodgy old fools aside. Daring, imaginative, innovative. Curing a new disease or inventing a new procedure. Driving a fine roadster and lecturing on my innovations at learned conferences. To be rich, successful, en-vied. To be at the pinnacle of my profession and to never look down.

"The Prime Minister's office issued a caution today against calling the current economic down-turn a depression."

"Love thy neighbour as thyself."

The ski-slopes north of Montréal. Only forty minutes by train. The snow is perfect and your skis never touch the ground.

He tilts his head back and x-rays the ceiling. Gotta let all this soak in. Never forget the name of the saint, that's for sure. "Giotto's *Life of St. Francis.* It's on the ceiling of the church." It was Frances who told him he'd like it. "It's right up your alley", is what she had said. They both laughed when he asked, "You're named after a saint?" A life in twenty-eight panels. Wearing a very drab, brown robe. The giving-away of his cloak. Turning his back on a bundle of rich-es. Banishing demons from peoples' lives. Water springing from a rock. Blood streaming from the wound in his side. They were buckling up their skis when she told him he'd have to see it. He had told her one of his thoughts. "As I was skiing down the side of the mountain, I got the strange idea that I'd like to become a monk!"

A mother counting pennies on a kitchen table.
A man putting a padlock on the door of a store.
The roof of a boxcar covered with men.

"Bethune lives every hour intensely. He is impatient with what I would call everyday life."

"Bethune's mind is a St. Catherine's wheel – always throwing off sparks in all directions. His mind is always working in double-time."

An infected finger - granted none of the liberties - a set of scales on his mantle - torn and perfumed fragment - a tiny crust of bread - an arctic explorer - hunted animals - other tides, other oceans - to achieve a meeting of minds - overrun with choking weeds.

Brewed inside an egg like everyone else. Nurtured in primeval fluid like a duckling or a swan. Eager for a chance to swim downstream.

My father was a Presbyterian minister. My mother was a missionary. I went to Sunday School and church twice every Sunday.

I come from a race of men who are widely-travelled. A drop of family blood nurtures many a far-flung thorn. No Bethune has ever been known to compromise.

It was Young Proffit's first day on the job.
He was the son of the President of the Conglomerate.
He was now Vice-president of Everything That His Father Owned.

Building up a practice. Making an impact in a town. A busy, growing city. Full of rewards for the young and ambitious. An office in a busy part of the inner-city. High walls hung with paintings. A sprinkling of diplomas. A client list which grows by leaps and bounds. A Voluntary Assistantship in the Department of Surgery in the Out-patients' Division of the Hospital. Trading lore, testimonials and influence with the other doctors. Part-time Instructor in Prescription Writing in the Department of Pharmacology and Therapeutics. Lectures on medicine as a noble profession. A call to the highest levels of human endeavour. The practice of medicine as a modern priestly craft.

"The President declared today that economic conditions are basically sound and that the fundamental strength of the economy is unimpaired."

Renting an apartment.
Checking out the price of a new roadster.

Two people melting together.

The fragments of a shattered vase.
An eagle perched on a nest.

He sits at a table on the sidewalks of Paris. Everyone chatting. Plenty of drinkers; plenty of drinks. Not one of them has bothered to mention the War. They think of me as the life of the party. Always the quip and the fun idea. "Let's grab us some bottles of wine and go see Muldoon!" Those poor buggers didn't have to die. Lots of them still had a chance to live. They were alive when we rolled them onto the stretcher; they were dead when we rolled them off. The girls cackle and the men chortle. They plead with the waiter for another round of drinks. "We were here first! We're your best customers! We beg you – please!" A scene right out of Dante: The Stygian Stretcher-bearer Service. Alive on the stretcher; dead on delivery. This café could have been a lot more crowded. So many of those poor bastards didn't have to die.

A hundred workers answering an ad for ten jobs.
A car being pulled by a horse.
Family furniture out on the sidewalk on rent day.

He is a breath of fresh air in the medical profession.
He is the man who is setting medicine on its ear.

A stunning mountain view - all that you have - back from the dead - only healed scars - an extremely difficult procedure - rehearsing your final words - the negative and the positive - the value of herbs - continue to rain death - race with the clock.

I served in the trenches of France in 1915. Mud, blood, burnt lungs and splintered bones. The face turns white as the ground turns red with blood.

I dawdled in the cafés of Paris. Forty miles from the agony, the mud and the blood. Turn your back on the scars of the War and have a drink.

Post-war studies at the Hospital for Sick Children in St. Ormond Street. Eager to tilt against the champions of infantile disease. To make a name for myself amid the profession's elite.

Pestilence sat alone with his drink in a tavern.
Outside the window, his white horse munched his oats.
I have tried to infect War but to no avail.
I need a less-formidable foe to destroy.

Treating patients in my home. Letting the secretary go. Without an office, I couldn't justify keeping her on. Asking Frances to answer the door, but it's not for her. I enjoy teaching at the college. Like to keep it relaxed and real. We walk past breadlines to get to the campus. Asking the students what they have noticed on the way to class. What does this tell you of the state of medicine at the present time? Like to give their heads a shake and hear them rattle. Not all students take to my lectures. Some of them think of me as a Lefty. One of them had me called on the carpet as a Commie one time. One of them told me, sotto voce, that his father is a doctor, and he had never – even once – thought of medicine as a noble profession, or of serving the public at a sacrifice to oneself. To his father, it's all about climbing the ladder of wealth.

A dark cave. An infant. A red pterodactyl. Long teeth, sharp fangs, bat-like wings. A baby is attacked in a cave.

Was it Frances or was it me? Impossible – not even desirable – to assign fault. Not for nobility – but for accuracy – I accept all blame.

Do you see yourself as an iconoclast?
What moulds do you wish to break?
Will you break the moulds or will the moulds break you?

Facing a mountain of debts. Oh to be a doctor without a conscience. To climb the ladder by stepping on hands. I treat everyone who needs me. Never turn a patient away. I ask for little money and often get none. Good books, good paintings, good wines. Entertaining friends and colleagues. All of these cost money. I tell Frances over and over: Sure there's a Depression, but what are we working for if once in a while we can't have a little fun? Should a doctor be taking the streetcar? Where's the dignity in that? Arriving with my shoes all spotted and mud down the leg of my pants? You don't build a practice by stripping your life to the bones!

"Business leaders have repeatedly asserted that the recent dip in employment figures is merely a temporary measure which will help to stabilize the economy."

"From each according to his abilities; to each according to his needs."

A girl with the scent of heather in her hair.
A man painting a picture late at night.
A horse munching oats outside a tavern.

The porch light is yellow. It shines on an anguished face. He pulls the door open and a man flinches as if he expects to be met with anger. He holds his hand up – with a wrinkled dollar – in front of his chest. "My wife is going into labour. I didn't know where to take her. She's in a boxcar with two of our kids. Someone said you might help." He takes the dollar out of the man's hand, folds it and stuffs it in the pocket of the man's shirt. "Put your dollar away. Your money's no good here. How far along is she now?" He steps aside and holds the door open. "Come in. It's cold out there. Come in while I get my things. She's in a boxcar? That means there's no heat. No running water either. If there's time, we'll take her to the hospital in my car. At any rate, we'll do the best we can."

Relief trains carrying turnips, bread and cod.
Picking over the trash at the city dump.
Lines for soup kitchens stretching around the block.

"Bethune's students have a high opinion of him. He sees medicine as a modern priestly craft."

"Bethune is very egotistical and driven by a demon. He wants to be a hero or a martyr at any cost."

A cup turned upside down - holding an x-ray up to the light - the glow of one's whole life - mission aborted; credit denied - suckling a child - the centre of the world - a meeting place for ideas - the locomotives of history - a tangle of mis-matching languages - a numbed face.

My father and my mother were a great influence on my life. I fought with my father all the time. With my mother, I had no quarrel at all.

We met in Scotland, Frances and I, after the War. She was not like me and I was not like her. Her mother warned her not to marry a man like me.

So I didn't get along with Dr. Archibald? So who was right and who was wrong? I tried to pull him up out of the mud, but he wouldn't budge.

Three men met at an inn.
They were tired and they were dusty.
The servant had already washed their feet.

Working long and tiring hours. I never refuse a call. None of my clients has any money. If one of them does, I always make him pay through the nose. It all averages out in the end: those who have a dollar pay for those who have none. Gas in the car, pills or salve, maybe fifty cents for a meal. My pocket gets emptied every time I make a call. Frances wonders why I don't simply say I won't go. I know I haven't been good for her. Invest some money in a sure-fire scheme; buy a new car. These are boosts that I need to fight the exhaustion and despair. There is nothing for her here. My practice is swirling down the drain. I built a castle for my love with her family legacy. Every penny that Frances inherited is just about gone.

"For those who have money the present economic situation can be looked on as good news indeed. You can buy a beautiful McIntosh apple for a single cent."

Setting an arm.
Sewing up a wound.

A man on his first day on the job.
Two love-birds dancing to the sound of a gramophone.
A scroll with an inventory of the world.

She clutches a little red purse. So small it seems as if it belongs to her child. Perhaps it does. Perhaps that's all she has to keep her money in. "Do you know the word 'tuberculosis'? Do you understand what that means?" She doesn't indicate one way or another. "It's caused by substandard living conditions." Her face is as blank as blank. She doesn't seem as if she understands. She squeezes the purse in her hands. She looks around at the child who is lying, still, on the couch. The child is breathing steadily. The chest slowly rises and falls. A long deep sleep would do her some good right now. "Is your husband coming home soon?" She clutches the purse tighter still. Small and silk and red. Little tassels that used to be gold, or maybe white. "Oh – money. Is that what you're thinking? No. What I gave her is yours for free. You don't need your purse. It doesn't matter what you can pay. I'll leave some more here, in this bottle, for when she wakes up. A teaspoonful in water and have her drink it slowly, not in a gulp." The little red purse between us, clutched in her hands. "I think your girl will be all right. She just needs time and sleep. Can you make the water hot? It will help to dissolve the syrup. Have you any more coals for the fire? Will your husband be coming home soon? Is he at work?"

Men wearing placards asking for work.
Empty hospital beds for lack of paying customers.
A tractor ploughing as the topsoil blows in the wind.

He is the doctor with a heart of gold.
His compassion for his fellows knows no bounds.

Gods of ourselves - a series of problems - no shortage of agony - struggle back into life again - to dive all the way down - a cat on the train - a wall of books - good and fine and free - more alive than other people - pain over my heart.

There were children hunting for coals along the railway track. They would gather them in a sack. They would take them home for their parents to heat the house.

I saw medicine as the noblest of professions. The Knights of the Scalpel, the Knights of the X-ray, the Knights of the Rib-shears. The Knights of the Bed-pan I would say, when I needed a laugh.

What kind of country is this? Is this a society without a soul? Is every person just a separate lump of clay?

A voice spoke to the doctor in a dream.
Physician, heal thyself! the voice said.
Oh, I can do that, the doctor replied.
I shall add an extra dollar to all of my fees.

I don't know what to think about Frances. Dragging her around like this. Dropping her down in a strange town and expecting her to fend for herself. It's a long way from Scotland and family. It's a long way from our honeymoon for sure. Used to ask her what she did all day, but haven't asked her for a while. Tough to ring her up on the phone and tell her that tonight I'll be slightly delayed. Hard to break away from the hospital. No such thing as medicine on a schedule. Buy her something as compensation – a painting or a vase – and it causes a row. You should be paying the heat and hydro. You should be saving for a rainy day. With you the bills are always the last things to be paid.

A mud hut on the edge of a village.

The ebb and flow of the seasons.
The sun's eye watching us all day.
The cycle of the days and months and years.

A carpenter planes a piece of wood.

A Roman doctor visiting a villa. Checking a man whose eyes are blind.
You will see when I remove these cataracts.

Another stops to chat and they whisper their words.

Does the dye subdue the hand?
Does the hand subdue the dye?
Where, in this equation, is the cloth?

Shortness of breath. This has never happened before. At times I can barely drag myself through the day. Put it off for a couple of weeks. Mind over matter. Never known it to happen before. Always think of myself as a workhorse. Maybe the stress about paying the bills. Long days and longer evenings. Never a night to relax at home. Frances isn't the easiest person to live with, though mind you she often says the same about me. Can't seem to get through the day. Can't deny that it's getting worse. Examined by a colleague. Collar open, shirt removed. A tap on the chest and a cough. An x-ray of the lungs. Tuberculosis of moderate extent. Sanitarium treatment. Great strides have been made of late. Favourable outlook for recovery if all goes well. That's ridiculous! I'm the doctor! I can't afford to abandon all this! I've barely gotten started on my career!

Chapter 2

Canada 2

The Trudeau Sanitarium. Saranac Lake, New York. Twenty-eight cottages. Two infirmaries. Library. Laboratory. Medical and reception pavilions, therapy workshop, nurses' home, chapel and post office. Acres of pine-covered slopes on the side of a mountain. Two hundred staff, one hundred and sixty beds. Pulmonary tuberculosis. Fresh air and complete rest. In bed for at least a month. Short walks and shortness of breath. Benches along the walkways for us to sit down. Day after day they tell me I am improving. Day after day I sit and think. Life is a farce and I am a futile figure in it. A disease for which there is no known cure? A disease which one can live with? Not a mode of living at all. There are patients here who have been in bed for over a year.

Money, fame, prestige.

Two people melting together.
A firing squad firing a volley of shots.
A man plunging a needle into his chest.

Success, roadster, art.

A shady grove in ancient India. Reading from an Ayurveda text. Diseases, their diagnosis and expected cures.

A practice with diplomas on the wall.

Why do you want fine wines and a roadster?
Why crave the respect of those you despise?
How much money was in your pockets the day you were born?

Accepting the fact that I'll soon be dead. Painting a mural. The story of my life. Around the walls of the cottage. On sheets of wrapping paper which I found in the laundry room. Five feet high and sixty feet long – all four sides of the cage. Nine panels in all – each panel a stage in my aborted life. Sirens and bats and castles and rocks. Cities and rivers and blood. Sputum cups and angels. Pterodactyl and Spanish galleon. A false Hollywood set and a rocky abyss. Dipping my brush in a can on the table. Slathering paint as I stand on a chair. Once in a while a pause, while I cough up a part of a lung. I put my cell-mates in the mural. A tombstone for each one. We have all outlived our days. We are all condemned to die. What we are doing here is a very slow dance of death. I give myself five years. I paint on my tombstone: 1932.

"One million Canadians are now on public relief."

"Medicine heals doubts as well as diseases."

Oh, there are many types of snow, but fresh clean powder is best of all. The skis bite clean and you get your best speed. There is nothing like skiing downhill on a sunny day.

He is sitting on a cardboard box in a large room. Rows of suitcases stacked on shelves. Scattered and opened cardboard boxes are strewn on the floor. *Do you remember the room with its parapets of books?* He has his clip-board on his knee and he scribbles words on the pages of a prescription pad, pausing to number each one before he tears it off and drops it down beside him. *I would like just to see you tonight and hold your hand for an hour in a garden.* He yawns. It is late at night. There is still one favourite book that he must find. *I will write you later in the week and tell you all.* Cold coffee in a cup. A pile of prescription notes on the floor. He is sitting in his overcoat. The unheated room is extremely cold.

Bread lines on the sidewalk.
Hoboes riding the rails.
Children begging pennies on the street.

"Bethune is a bad drinker. When he drinks, he becomes irascible and difficult."

"Bethune is a man of great obsessions. Whenever he drinks, he mumbles about his wife."

The peaceable society - the levers of power - so raw and so bleeding - a faceless crowd - emptied of delight - superior mind in a crisis - abandoned the common man - the logic of a bayonet - the role of the dollar - life slowly slipping away.

Floating in a sack of amniotic fluid. Thinking thoughts about the waiting unknown. Dreaming the dreams that are the nectar of the soon-to-be-born.

Religion to me was not so much attendance at church. Or praying for our souls to go to heaven. Rather the Bible as a catalogue of the sufferings of the world.

A citizen of Canada; a citizen of the world. Normandy, Scotland, Hawaii. The family roots drink from the waters at the ends of the earth.

The great god rubbed his temples as he thought of his problem.
He had built himself a world and it had gone wrong.
Infinity weighed on his shoulders like a two-pail yoke.

Evading the nurses' patrol. Barnwell and I stuffing our ski-jackets with blankets and pillows. Propping our surrogates in our beds. Sneaking out the cottage window. Past the night-watchman and down the path to the town. An evening in the tavern. A few laughs and a glass of wine. Gathering around the piano and singing old songs. Making up lyrics about what the nurses would say if they found our corpses lying so still in our beds. Watching our breath drift away in the moonlight as the stars sparkle overhead outside the tavern. The snow crunching beneath our boots as we walk back from town. Sneaking into our rooms. Up the side of the cottage and in through the window again. Beating the system as much as we can, if only by inches. Like the boys from the trenches on leave. Let us eat, drink and be merry, for tomorrow we may die. Tomorrow we certainly die – the odds are printed in the medical books and everyone knows that statistics never lie.

"World trade has declined by more than fifty percent."

Stretcher-bearing in the trenches in 1915.
Drinking in a café in Paris after the war.

A man hearing a voice in a dream.
A man lying on a bed and staring at the ceiling.
The fragments of a shattered vase.

He wipes his forearm on the window and makes an opening in the frost. Snow swirls around the tiny porch and covers the path. No sign of the side of the mountain in the blurring snow. He turns around and considers the room. Four of us living in this tiny cottage. One sitting in the armchair in his three-piece suit and reading a days-old newspaper. "Would you believe that another bank has had to foreclose?" One lying on his bed in the bathrobe that he has worn both night and day, with his eyes firmly shut, slowly rubbing his temples. "Looks like there's going to be no end to this snow." One sitting at the table, open-neck shirt and tennis shoes, and scratching a letter, the open inkwell dangerously close to his sleeve. "Same symptoms as I mentioned a week ago." He turns back to the window and watches the swirling snow.

A job that pays twenty-seven cents per day.
School teachers working for board rather than pay.
Auto workers trying to form an illegal union.

He is highly critical of current medical procedures.
He is defiant in the face of death as he approaches his end.

A well-tuned clock - to measure gold and silver - stabbed in the back - the sick, the halt and the lame - a fountain spouting blood - his personal fief - no heroes and no villains - wars and rumours of wars - every tenet by which he lives - disdain for familiar pathways.

The men would gurgle on the stretchers. Lean over and spit up blood. We would carry them back from the Front as fast as we could.

There was war and there was peace. The war was a puddle of blood on a stretcher. The peace was a gallon of wine in a Paris café.

Learning contempt for the staid and the stodgy. Eager to break the routines of disease. Chafing in my role as a lowly intern.

The leader saluted and began his oration to the troops.
We shall bomb their troops in the field.
We must do this for the cause.
It is essential to achieve our victory.

I don't want to die. Like those boys who went over the trenches in the War. Every one of them felt that there was something in him that meant that he was the one who should make it through the nightmare-barrage and go on living. Many of them were wrong, of course, but some of them knew they had something inside them that was bound to keep them alive. Some wore a Bible over their hearts or a silver cigarette case, but others felt that there was something deeper inside that was proof against bullets, bombs and disease. I know I am one of those men. I'll come out of the trenches alive. I have too much life left to live. I am one of those who has willed himself not to die.

A girl. Apple cheeks. Ruddy complexion. The scent of heather in her hair. The girl and her young man, arm in arm. A freshet chuckles cheerfully through the glen.

The honeymoon trip to Paris – and the rest of Europe. Idly tossing her legacy onto the fire in a fancy chalet. Buying art when Frances thought I was buying food.

What is it like to be so close to death?
Is death a bloody maw or a pair of mocking eyes?
What is the one thing that you wish that you had done?

Reading everything that has been written about tuberculosis. Neglected books in the Sanitarium library. *Tuberculosis. Formerly called consumption. An infectious disease of the lungs. Spread through the air by those who have an active infection, by coughing or sneezing. Kills more than fifty percent of those who are infected. There is no known cure. Chronic bed-rest is always recommended* ... Leafing through the books that I've spread on the table. What's this one all about? An article on artificial pneumothorax treatment – artificial collapse of the lung. Skimming the pages and shouting Eureka! Sticking a piece of paper between the pages! Signing the book out at the desk! Hurrying over to the infirmary! Asking to speak to the medical doctors on staff!

"Twenty-six point six percent of all wage-earners are unemployed."

"Communists are like seeds and the people are like the soil."

Stricken soldiers gurgling on stretchers.
A baby thinking thoughts as he waits to be born.
A god rubbing his temples and trying to think.

He lies on the bed. On top of the covers. Still in his slippers and his robe. A sliver of light shines through the curtain and across his legs. *As if I am sleeping in a cave.* He leans back against the pillows. At times like this, I used to take a puff on a cigarette, the ashtray on the night-table filled with ashes and a few squashed butts. Beside me, my wife would lie, breathing as steadily as a mummy, in her cocoon. I used to check the alarm clock by the glow of my cigarette. *As if the bats are my ideas. Coming and going in the night as I try to sleep.* I would be churning out ideas even as I was sleeping. I couldn't wait to get up to top speed at the break of day. I'd have a bundle of schemes all ready to put into practice. Now, the only real thought that I have is: "This cannot go on".

Neighbours protecting a family faced with eviction.
Women sewing piece-work at home for starvation pay.
A plague of grasshoppers destroying the prairie lands.

"Bethune has a domineering manner. He picks arguments and causes squabbles wherever he goes."

"Bethune is a man who ignores all obstacles. This makes him a terror for bureaucrats and a source of anxiety for his few friends."

A ripple effect - to hold ourselves responsible - stained with blood - the greatest breaker of hearts - a case of logic - back from the dead - a few kind words - the dictionary definition - fragments of thoughts - the slamming of a cup.

My father fought the demon in me that he feared in himself. I fought the demon in my father that I feared in me. When both of those demons were dead, we were both free to go.

When Frances and I first met, I felt that I had found the rest of myself. She was the fragment that had been missing from the moment of birth. I absorbed her into my skin and carried on.

Fear of change is a palpable fear. Better to stay with the tried and the true. I drove a roaster and Archibald rode in a rocking chair.

The people met in the courtyard during the day.
Their fellows were being attacked and eaten at night.
It seems to be a wolf, someone said.

You must think of yourself as a patient, Doctor Bethune. You are a general practitioner, not a specialist in tubercular treatment. Your own case is outside your area of medical expertise. Artificial pneumothorax treatment has been tried, as you have said, but it is a new and uncertain procedure. There are sure to be many risks involved. There is the use of a hollow needle. Have you considered what might go wrong? What if a lung is pierced by the needle? Complications would no doubt ensue and then where would we be? We are a respected institution. We are acknowledged as one of the best. We are known as a rest facility. You say you found this "cure" in a book? Not one of our doctors is willing to entertain such a risk. Excuse me, Doctor Bethune, but this is a serious medical discussion! Your levity is not at all welcome! Surely you are joking when you assert that you will operate on yourself!

"Two-thirds of the young people entering the work-force cannot find steady employment."

> Painting a farewell mural.
> Reading Communist literature.

> *A man forging a shield to cover his heart.*
> *A leader giving an oration to his troops.*
> *A man blowing the dust from library books.*

He sits down on a bench and looks up at the hills. It takes him a moment to catch his breath. Looks like perfect snow today. Excellent conditions for a day out on the slopes. Tubercular patients do not ski, of course. The lungs can't stand the strain. The cure for tuberculosis is to rest. Other patients take their places on the benches. Slow and steady; take frequent breaks; do not over-stress. This place is perfect. High up in the hills. Plenty of snow. He rises from the bench. His eyes sweep over the valley. Clear away a few trees and I could see a pretty-good ski-run, right over there. What would it take to turn this place into a ski-resort?

> *A job that pays three dollars and eighty cents a week.*
> *Transients lining the sidewalks of Vancouver.*
> *Politicians constantly promising relief.*

He is saving himself from death by tuberculosis.
He is determined that he will operate on himself.

> *Dry wells in a time of drought - what the day will bring - the dove and the scorpion - the union of life and death - the glue that binds us together - the finest cream - an unrealized dream - like diamonds under his feet - a man squeezing an orange - the poor will always be with you.*

Parents would tuck a blanket up around the neck of a sick child. They would dump their can of coins on the kitchen table. They would shuffle the coins and wonder what they could afford.

How did money ever come between doctor and patient? How did money manage to form such an inhuman wall? Pin their hand to the table with a scalpel and take their cash.

Why do old people beg on the street corners? Why are there children without enough food? Why is compassion not available to all?

> *A man had a set of scales on his mantle.*
> *A visitor asked him what the scales were for.*

My only regret is Frances. What a life I have thrust upon her. I offered to write a letter for her. To take back to Scotland to show to her family and friends. To explain that the fault was all mine. That I didn't appreciate her and treated her money as if it was trash. I got half-way through the letter and got off-track. I asked her if she remembered that little attic-room when we started out? How I got a hammer and saw and a few boards and a bag of nails and built us a book-case? Her novels and my medical books – a shelf for each? A glass of wine as we admired our handy-work? Two glasses of wine and we shuffled the books, so the novels and the medical books were side-by-side? Do you remember how we laughed? How we wondered if books can get pregnant? How we decided that surely they would if we let them drink wine?

A rocky gorge at the edge of a village.

A person absorbing another person into his skin.
A wolf prowling down alleys in the middle of the night.
A man skiing downhill on a perfect day.

The water tumbles and gurgles down.

Male and female healers among the Haudenosaunee. Setting bones, dressing wounds, performing surgery. Skilled in the use of plants and herbs.

As clear and clean as the snow that melts in the hills.

Blindfolded or facing the rifles?
Do you have a last meal in mind?
Have you spent much time rehearsing your final words?

The doctor – Dr. Warren. The patient – Norman Bethune. The operation – artificial pneumothorax treatment. Insert a hollow needle between the ribs. Pump air into the chest cavity. Put a cushion of air between the damaged lung and the chest wall. The lung then collapses and the progress of the disease is halted and the damaged lung is then allowed to rest. The operation is quite painless and should be repeated every week or two with a small needle. The spread of tuberculosis is halted and the lung will often heal. Bed-rest for a while, and soon the patient is up and about. Rest is still the cure, but now the lung is resting while the rest of the patient is allowed to go on with his life.

Chapter 3

Canada 3

Moving to Montreal. A lease on a new apartment and a new lease on life. A city of culture, vibrancy, hockey. Smoked meat and the finest of wines. With ski slopes forty miles north when the snow starts to fall. My health is excellent. An x-ray shows no disease – only healed scars. Appointed Chief Surgeon at the Royal Victoria Hospital by Dr. Archibald, whose specialty is pulmonary surgery. Part chest clinic and part research. When I told old Archy I was starving, he offered me a fellowship at fifteen hundred a year. The old fellow is a little stodgy, but so far we get along. As long as he lets me do what I want to do. I think I'll write a letter to Frances. She must be tired of her family by now. I'll ask her to come and join me in Montreal.

A tree swaying in the wind, a child at play, a bird in flight.

A girl with the scent of heather in her hair.
People drinking and talking far into the night.
A man with a set of scales on his mantel.

The sun falling on a numbed face like a benediction.

The inner and the outer in ancient China. The negative and the positive forces of energy. The need for a balance of yin and yang.

At times, to be alive is well enough.

Do you consider yourself more alive than other people?
Do you get the most out of every orange you squeeze?
What are your first thoughts to yourself as you start the day?

Making a centre of my apartment. A meeting place for ideas. Thoughtful chatter in the agora. Be sure to bring something to drink. A group of doctors from the hospital. A bunch of artists from the café. Liberals, Socialists, Communists. Pour into punch bowl – be sure to stir. A wall of books in my bookcase. Writers who shake up current ideas. Long discussions far into the night. The basis of a civilized society. The role of art in the x-rayed life. The role of medicine in the life of the community. The role of the dollar in our thoughts and in our lives. Taking up a collection. Whose turn to go out and get us more drinks? Sunday afternoons with the kids of the neighbourhood painting pictures. Marion Scott and Fritz Brandtner sharing their secrets. Lessons for free on the basics of painting. Trying to keep the apartment full. A lonely place without Frances. Taken best with a crowd of adults. Even better with kids.

"A mother who crochets baby jackets for a dollar sixty-five per dozen can never earn more than twenty-seven cents in a day."

"Workers of the world unite; you have nothing to lose but your chains."

Perfect ski weather is between minus six and minus one degree Celcius. Not so warm that the snow will melt but warm enough that you can stay on the slopes all day.

Sometimes they'll steal your shoes. While you're sleeping. That's why you sleep with your shoes underneath your head. Underneath your bindle, so nobody can steal your shoes while you're asleep. Anyway, nobody is going to steal anything here, he thinks, as he lies on top of a boxcar. He is staring at the stars, with his elbows hooked back down over the catwalk and the heels of his shoes – double-knotted – hooked over it too. My mom is very smart. She knew exactly where to sew the money so no one would ever think I had anything to steal. Her brother sent her the news. "Twenty dollars or I lose the farm. That's what they'll take for the taxes or they'll make me leave. If I can survive for one more winter, I think I'll be able to make it through. Please help if you can." The wind tears at his pant-legs. Flapping and snapping in the breeze. "You already have a patch on your knee," his mom explained. "You'll take the money to your uncle. I'll sew another patch on the inside. Inside the patch we'll put the money for the farm." I'll be farming with my uncle. He won't have to lose the farm. He stares up at the stars and thinks of his knee.

Protesters carrying placards asking for work.

Dust storms blackening the landscape.
Hoboes cooking at fires under bridges.

"There is no doubt that Bethune's bout with tuberculosis has deepened his intellectual and spiritual life. He wants to find something that he can do for the human race."

"Bethune always feels that he is right. He has no understanding of the other fellow's point of view."

Events on the world stage - the emotional subconscious - rescue the broken children - a weight on a chain - chatter in the marketplace - oh so much to do - one of my selves - we succeed as ideas - guarding the gates of a castle - working in a cave.

A woman in the agony of labour. A fountain spouting blood and milk and tears. Behind the blood, the significance of birth.

The blind, the lame, the lepers in the Bible. Similar suffering all around me as I walked to school. I sensed that we were living in Biblical times.

Beaverton, Blind River, Owen Sound. Gravenhurst, Toronto, Sault St. Marie. Me inside these places; they inside me.

A man and dog out walking in the woods.
They have long left the familiar path behind.
Each thinks his private thoughts as they walk along.

Spending hours in surgery. Spending hours in cafés. Spending hours at meetings, dances, parties. Feeling at odds and ends. Reading all kinds of books. Whatever anyone mentions as interesting. *The Present and Future Organization of Medicine, I Change Worlds, Moscow Dialogues, The Communist Manifesto, The Coming Struggle for Power, New Masses, New Frontier, Waiting for Lefty. The Oxford Book of English Verse* – William Blake. Writing all kinds of things. Whatever occurs to me in the middle of the night. Writing a little poetry – ... *the whole world is emptied of delight / Like a cup turned upside down.* Writing a radio play – *The Patient's Dilemma, or Modern Methods of Treating Tuberculosis.* Painting alone in the evenings. *Night Operating Theatre* – the operating room at the Sacré Coeur. A portrait in oils of Frances – by memory. *Self Portrait – 1935.* Someone remarking that there is pain and fear in the eyes. Talking with all kinds of people. Socialists and Communists and everyone in-between. The clash of social ideas. Finding more questions than answers. Is there anything other than science to put things right?

"Out-of-work Newfoundlanders receive six cents worth of food per day per member of the family."

Drawing diagrams of improved shears for cutting ribs.
Talking art with Marion over coffee.

A medical journal with a page of medical instruments.
A man designing an operation for a movie star.
Bread on sale for the price of jewels.

He sits on the park bench and scans the want-ads of the folded newspaper. Scanning like a chicken in search of a crumb. This morning, he'd made a mistake. Took the streetcar to the edge of town. Picked up by a truck as he held out his thumb. Didn't get to talk to the driver. Motioned to jump up into the back. There were two other fellows already packed into the cab. Breeze in his hair as he looked at the fields. What he could do with full-day's pay if he got this job. Couldn't believe it when they arrived. The two fellows from the cab of the truck got ahead of him in line. Seventeen men lined up at the gate. A couple of them eyed him up and down in his city-looking clothes. "Today we only need two. Hank and Bill, we'll take youse two. The rest of youse come back tomorrow an we'll see." It was a long walk back to the park. A blunt pencil had already worked-over the ads. Must already be close to noon. So much for day-old ads. The dime for the streetcar had been a mistake. A brand-new newspaper first thing this morning might have been a better buy.

Thin soup, a slice of bologna, a cup of tea.
Japanese armies invading Manchuria.
Banks refusing to lend and calling in loans.

He is a man by whom nothing is taken for granted.
He examines every thought in a balanced scale.

Comfy bags of money - a pile of arms and legs - turn on brothers - a society without a soul - a pretty good road - safe from the wolf - sacrifice for the cause - chaos in everything - among the debris - a mouthful of millet.

We would lean the stretchers upright against the wall. The men would blast them with a hose and let them dry. Impossible to clean off all the blood.

"Never again," was what we all said after the war. "There will be wars and rumours of wars" was wisely said too. What was it that could truly be "never again"?

Working hard and playing harder. Meeting the very best of the best. The rewards of making one's way to the top of the heap.

The physician was very proud of his ancient knowledge.

He laid out his instruments on a table of oak.
The stricken patient lay beside him as he prepared.

Pneumothorax Apparatus, complete with foot pump – the Nurse's Friend. The Bethune Scapula Lifter and Retractor – The Iron Intern. The Bethune Rib Strippers, The Bethune Rib Shears. The Bethune Thorascoscopic Scissors, rotatably mounted in handle; The Bethune Interpleural Clip Applying Forceps, including handle; The Bethune Silver Clips, for preventing hemorrhage; The Bethune Intercostal Trocar and Cannula, flat-oval; The Bethune Interpleural Transluminator, angles, use through trocar; The Bethune Connecting Cord, for use with the Transluminator; The Bethune Air-Tight Empyema Tube, with inflatable pneumatic collar for closed drainage, large or small; The Bethune Lobectomy Tourniquet, sliding pull; The Bethune Phrenectomy Necklace, for locating and masking post-operative scar; The Bethune Chest Charts, in sticker form, printed on gummed paper, in pads of fifty. Keeping the royalties from America. Giving the royalties for Canada to Masters. All I give him is my ideas – he does the rest.

An angel. Beautiful, with incandescent wings. Cloaked in long white flowing robes. Holding a baby in her arms. Another angel, unrolling a scroll and reading. Other angels, looking over his shoulder, turning away weeping.

Expecting Frances to live in Detroit. Far from the heather and the highlands and the mist. The two divorces were divorces from more than just me.

Why did you survive the tubercular trenches?
Do you think you deserved a reprieve?
What is the point of the gift of a second life?

What's going on here in Canada? We have a preventable epidemic. Forty-eight thousand people contract tuberculosis every year. Poverty, poor food, unsanitary conditions, contact with infectious foci, overwork, mental fatigue. Ask the banker if these are conditions which can be changed. My patients have no jobs. One tenth of the workers in Canada are unemployed. They live on government handouts of a dollar and twenty cents a week – eighty cents per child. There is a rich man's tuberculosis and a poor man's tuberculosis. Medicine is practised as a luxury trade. We sell bread at the price of jewels. Most people can't afford to stay alive. They huddle, shivering, under blankets when I visit them in their homes. A few kind words and some wise advice. A skinny hand reaching out with two or three coins. Their situations remain unchanged. I look them in the eyes and know they will die. Their agony is contagious. When one of them dies, a part of me dies too.

"Many young men are employed in relief camps, where they break rock, cut brush and push wheelbarrows of soil for twenty cents a day."

"Where the broom does not reach, the dust will not vanish of itself."

A doctor and a group of nuns sharing a laugh.
A man and a dog each thinking his private thoughts.
A man painting a self-portrait late at night.

"Fifty percent, you say? Fifty percent? Why not choose seventy-five or even a hundred?" Tossing the clip-board on the table. Almost hitting the coffee cups. One of the doctors pulls his cup away just in time. "Just because it works doesn't mean we can afford it! And you admit that it doesn't work every time! You said yourself it's overcrowding, malnutrition – everything else that comes with poverty! The sooner you send them out, they'll come right back in! 'The home of the incurables! Where people are sent to die!' I don't like people thinking like this any more than you do! But can you do it safely and efficiently? Can you do it with no extra staff?" One of the doctors picks up the carafe and re-fills the cups. "It's easy to play it all up in the journals, but this is the place where it has to work. There are five hundred beds in this place and every one is full. All you've really tried it on is just yourself!" The other doctors don't say a word. They're thinking here we go again. These two always like to go at it hammer and tong. Heavy breathing. Some moments of silence while coffee is being sipped. Then, the slamming of a cup down hard on the tray.

Panhandlers fighting against their self-respect.
A job that pays twelve dollars a week.
Thirty-eight measly cents for a bushel of wheat.

"Bethune is a man of egotistical stunts. He operates quickly just to break a record for time or to show up Dr. Archibald."
"Bethune's compassion for his patients is deep and moving. I have seen him sit by a bedside all night and hold a patient's hand."

The pressure of thought - no known cure - a man of moral integrity - a master-stroke of international diplomacy - how things went wrong - the depth of the soul - the history of class struggles - instantaneity of insight - a cup turned up-side down - constant pain in my heart.

My mother a missionary. "Others first; yourself last." At times I envied her that she was never in search of herself.
When Frances and I divorced the first time, I was glad to let her go. She was the part of me that needed to break away. There was a war inside myself that

needed a truce.

Dr. Archibald hired me because I reminded him of himself when he had been young. When he fired me, he was probably thinking exactly the same. Liberation or capitulation; life is war against the self; the self we murder must not be allowed to die in vain.

A light shone on the peak of a mountain.
A peasant watched it as it glowed.
Every night, he watched the light.
He watched it for the rest of his life.

I'm thinking of changing hospitals. The nuns at the Sacred Heart Hospital have their charms. They are looking for a surgeon to head up their new tubercular unit. Frequent clashes with Old Archy at the Royal Vic. He thinks I take risky cases when I operate and lose too many lives. I think he never takes risks when he decides whether or not to operate and gains no lives at all. We tell each other so almost every day. I take a broom to the old and the stodgy. The old and stodgy always object. I can't believe that the old ways of thinking are so entrenched.

"Canada is burning wheat. Alabama is ploughing-under cotton. Florida is dumping oranges into swamps. Brazil is dumping coffee into the ocean."

Fixing a cleft palate.
Setting a leg-bone.

A man writing a letter in an empty room.
A man squeezing an orange as the sun comes up.
Children painting pictures of Montreal.

He sits in the common room and sips at a cup of coffee. He flips through a medical journal with some of his own inventions inside. The ads present the medical world in a rosy glow. Unable to sleep last night. Back to work, early each morning, as if I'd never gone home. *I cannot sleep while the world is as it is.* One more cigarette and a sip of coffee and a glance out the window. *I must rise early and do what I can do.* Some of the doctors grab a few minutes of shut-eye in the common room. *I must bring some kind of relief to those in pain.* How they can put their minds in neutral, in the midst of this turbulent maelstrom, is unknown to me.

Long lineups at the Relief Office.
Dry wells in a time of drought.
Bankers riding to work in limousines.

He is a man who is shaking up his profession.
He turns a microscope on every single thought.

*The world in turmoil - plunging into an abyss - not used to measure gold
- part of your marrow - two swans gliding together - odour of burning wood - the
story of my life - the blessings of the gods - the pinnacle of my profession - the
soul, the body, the mind.*

There were doctors who couldn't pay their electrical bills. Medicine as a
business: service for pay. How can you deal with people who don't have a thing
to trade?

When I look a parent in the eye I see dollar signs. When he looks me in
the eye he sees dollars too. We ignore the child in agony on the couch.

Why are there mothers afraid to call for a doctor? Why do young men
sleep on park benches? What is the force that makes the children's paintings so
dark?

*In the beginning, I made a world, said God.
I made it with the calipers in my hand.
I created the heavens and the earth.
Everything I made, I made of chaos;
There is chaos in everything I made.*

Writing long letters to Frances, some of which I never send. Turning
some of them into thoughts about my thoughts. *A theory of art ... the ratio-
nal mind ... imposing discipline and order ... seeming chaos and seeming disorder ... the emotional subconscious ... appetite for life ... the depths of another
world ... leviathan of the deep ... all-embracing eye ... dark ancestry ... new
birth.* Beth-babble, Beth-babble, Beth-babble. Thoughts about thoughts about
thoughts. The great artist playing ping-pong against himself. But what have
these thoughts to do with you? Miss you and wish you all the best. My apartment
is always filled with laughter. Hope the same is true for you. Remember those
laughs we had when we lost control of our skis?

Darkness in the village.

*Two people arguing loudly with drinks in their hands.
A physician laying out his instruments.
A man sitting in an armchair reading a book.*

The moon is not visible in the sky.

An operation on a patient in ancient Israel. A doctor drills a hole in a patient's skull. The only way to relieve inter-cranial pressure.

Stars shine, but not enough to light the way.

Why do you think of Frances and the ditch-debacle?
Why do you think of Frances and the errant skis?
Why do you think of the times when the two of you were one?

Don't tell me Canada has failed! How can you think such a thing! Canada is growing! Don't write her obituary yet! She's young and still unformed! A Garden of Eden still unploughed! Old Laurier was right! The Twentieth Century belongs to Canada! Look at these kids as they work on their paintings! They don't want to hear you talk like that! Put your cynicism aside and roll up your sleeves! You can sit inside and complain about the weather, or you can go outside and shovel snow! What we need is organization! The people who run things are smarter than we are! The drug they dispense is the drug of ideas! We all know what Canada needs! The same as any other country! Most of the others are too far gone! I could agree with you if we weren't living in Montréal! Here. Look. Let's settle down. Talk is cheap; work is hard. Let's drop this whole conversation. I have a few things in mind, but tonight is for fun. In the meantime, have another drink and watch the kids. That's what I'm going to do. In their art you can see the future – both good and bad. Their art is asking us what their future is going to be.

Chapter 4

Canada 4

Plunging myself into life. Spent a wonderful day today. Up at nine, toast and coffee and delicious marmalade. A walk along Sherbrooke Street to the hospital. Clinical work until one. Research from two to three. Home to bed until six. Then up and make myself dinner and paint or read. In the evenings, go to a film or a hockey game. On the weekends, a train to the ski hills. Down to the station for 8:35. Forty miles and I'm on the slopes again. I can ski six miles in a day. Eat my lunch from a pack on my back. Be back in the station and home again by nine. If I didn't have a conscience, I could nap like a cat on the train. Why can't my patients have the life that I get to lead?

A lump of coal squeezed in the hand produces a diamond.

A man on a train waxing his skis.
A free clinic with a line-up out to the street.
A visitor peering inside an open door.

That is what an artist does with a painting.

Viking villagers toil in the sunshine in the herb garden. Grateful that the spring has come at last. Burdoch, Vervain, Ground Ivy, Mayweed, Plantain.

That is what a person can do with his life.

Are you a man who lives best alone?
Is that your self-portrait there on the wall?
Would you say that the background resembles a faceless crowd?

Opening a free clinic. Every Saturday at noon. Free to women and children and the unemployed. Climbing the heights of the medical establishment. Writing papers, inventing new instruments, developing new procedures. Joining the American Association of Thoracic Surgery. Elected to their five-man council. An up and coming young man in the medical field. Presenting papers that breed opposition. Upsetting the apple cart. Taking on the sacred Brahmins. Your operations are a success, but they produce impressive statistics by leaving the worst of your patients alone to quietly die. Becoming enraged at my own profession. Resistance builds each time I speak. The hands on the tiller are not about to let go.

"In Montréal, twenty-thousand protesters marched along St. Catherine Street to protest the ineffectiveness of the government's efforts to combat current economic conditions."

"In bourgeois society, capital is independent and has individuality, while the living person is dependent and has no individuality."

Some skiers put the scenery ahead of the snow conditions. Too bad for them if they have to make a choice. The true ski afficionado makes certain of both.

Her name is Marion and she is a painter. She is mixing paint at the sink. Fritz Brandtner, the other painter, distributes the brushes. A spacious flat, a large front room. A kitchen a few steps up and a balcony where the sunflowers grow in pots. The children are spread around the room, each working alone. Large pieces of paper and paint-pots, here and there, of many colours. The alleys, the streets, the smoke, the smells. Marion moves around the room. Listening more than talking. Approving more than instructing. The parks, the skies, the moon. Occasionally, a rainbow. No coaching from the parents. Let them be free to explore their thoughts. Let them be free to explore their emotions. Take your drinks out on the balcony. Let the children have their own moment – let them be. Marion's eyes flash as she shoos the parents away.

Feeding a family on six cents per person per day.

Nurses sent home for lack of a paycheque.
Free clinics overwhelmed with those in need.

"Bethune's individuality is superficial. His unconventional clothes and his flouting of social conventions are proof of that."

"Bethune is innovative in his medical theory, technique and inventiveness. Whether redesigning an instrument or painting a picture, he is his own man."

A lump of coal - what's best for us all - sunshine, clouds, blue skies, a gentle rain - a definite proposal - the power to cut through rock - bearing the brunt - a very slow dance of death - all of the pesky flies - what I have learned - never touch the ground.

Am I an amoeba to throb unnoticed? Am I a crustacean to scour the seas? Am I an eagle, ready to launch myself into the air?

Not so much the Christ on the cross. More the Christ who walked among us. The Christ who healed the sick, the halt and the lame.

Yearning for the freedom of open water. Sensing that I am anchored in a cove. Smelling the breezes that insistently tug at my sails.

Two workers were standing and talking in the lobby.
Hello, Young Proffit! one of them called.
Welcome to your first day on the job!

Reading far into the nights. Milk and a sandwich beside my chair. Marx's *Communist Manifesto*. Engels's *Socialism: Scientific and Utopian*. Lenin's *The State of the Revolution*. Plekhanov's *On the Role of the Individual in Society* as well. Talking to people who have been to Russia. What is going on over there? What do they mean by A Worker's Paradise! Did you get inside a hospital? What is their medical system like? How do we know that they have all the answers? Bolshie baloney or genuine progress? Their leaders are masters of propaganda, just like ours!

"Thousands of unemployed are marching on Ottawa in an effort to convince the Federal Government to do something about the plight of the unemployed."

Popping a letter to Frances in the mailbox.
Arguing endlessly about social issues.

A hand on the tiller of a boat.
A peasant watching a light which glows on a mountain.

A group of people talking around a table.

Late at night. Operating theatre. Montreal. A woman with a tumour in the lower abdomen. Too dangerous for the doctors in Hartford. Not willing to take the risk. So she came to me. A long and complicated operation. I always start with the time that is on the clock. A surgeon is a craftsman and an artisan. A craftsman with the soul of the creative artist. Bound by the rigid and inexorable laws of the human body. Granted none of the liberties of those who work in wood or metal or stone. I work as quickly as I can. To shorten the time under anaesthesia and to reduce the force of the shock. Important to keep things moving. If I don't win my race with the clock, she could lose a leg.

Working in a restaurant for six dollars a week plus meals.
People dying needlessly of tuberculosis.
The unemployed sleeping in bunks in St. Lawrence Hall.

He is a man who is impatient with worn-out ideas.
He is a man who is constantly renewing himself.

The waiting unknown - pressing news - the need I saw - blackened walls and roofless beams - to realize an ideal - into the mouth of hell - everyday life - a better way to do it - chants and gongs and bells - the depths of his soul.

If you could keep the blood inside, the man would live. If it all leaked out on the stretcher, the man would die. That was the dictionary definition of life and death.

Idle chatter about how the post-war world was so wounded. About the great works of art we were going to write and paint. One more drink and you would be sure that you could do both.

Tasting the very best that life on earth has to offer. Sampling fine wines and engaging in clever repartee. Acquiring a penchant for the taste of the finest cream.

War sat alone with his drink in a tavern.
Outside the window, his red horse munched his oats.
I have tried to stab Famine but to no avail.
I need a less-formidable foe to destroy.

Turning down an offer from the Communists. To serve as the Head of the Friends of the Soviet Union. Not convinced that they have all the answers. Agree that capitalism has failed! Agree with the public funding of health care! But what about personal freedoms! What do the Communists say about that? Isn't it really just one more religion? The same as all the others have been?

Start out offering change and then the next thing you know things are worse than they've ever been! Are you sure things are better in Russia? How could we possibly know? Listen! This is Montreal! Quebec! Canada! Better to talk about changes at home! No future for Communism here! Look, if I joined the Communist party, my voice would never be heard! It's hard enough to get them to listen now! Even the parties seem to get snarly. Is it the drink or is it just me?

Out walking in the heather. A girl and her young man. Beside the trail, the young man jumps a ditch. You must follow me, he says. You must do as I have done. You must jump the ditch as I have done or I shall never have respect for you again.

Expecting Frances to jump the ditch. What in the world could I have been thinking? Something died in me when she refused to jump.

Why so often these thoughts of Frances?
Isn't she better left in the past?
Do we drag our past around like a weight on a chain?

Is the whole world on fire? A civilization in crisis. Breadlines on the streets. People dying of preventable illnesses. Doctors holding out their hands for coins that just aren't there. Fanatics appealing to the masses – in Germany, Italy and Spain. The people who run our society reclining on comfy bags of money and sending police against the people who ask for bread. Skiing and partying in the maelstrom! How long can this go on! Operating, reading, talking, thinking! Drinking, painting, walking, arguing! Giving my salary to the poor! Cans of paint on my dining room carpet! The children painting their hopes and their fears! Sometimes I feel like my head is about to explode! Out of the blue, a chance to see something that interests me – an offer to travel to Russia to see their medical system in operation. The International Physiological Congress in St. Petersburg.

"Seventeen thousand people filled Maple Leaf Gardens in Toronto to cheer for Tim Buck, the leader of the Communist Party of Canada."

"The people, and the people alone, are the motive force in the making of world history."

A man enjoying coffee and toast and marmalade.
A man staggering in a desert with a staff in his hand.
An operating theatre with a quickly-moving clock.

He takes a sip from his glass and places it on the windowsill. He rubs the frost away from the widow and leans over and looks at the street. *The beating of my heart.* The snow is drifting down. There will be skiing up in the hills. Perhaps on Saturday. *The whole world is emptied of delight.* The adults and children have all gone home. Paintings left on the floor to dry. One could look at them for hours with glass in hand. *A cup turned upside down.* He thinks and thinks and thinks. The snow, the paintings – other things. *I can't pretend this happens every day.* Wonder where my life is going to take me now?

> *Fishing boats tied to the docks.*
> *A street full of vacant houses.*
> *The outbreak of civil war in Spain.*

"Dr. Bethune is always asking what he should read. He has an amazing instantaneity of insight."

"Bethune is a restless soul. He is looking for something which, so far, he hasn't found."

Brewed inside an egg - a single drop of water - an iroquois healer - built himself a world - the well-intentioned attempt - the peace of mind of a grazing mule - lost without me - they'll shred our forces - clothing in a vat - looking into your soul.

Visits with my siblings were always a pleasure. Good people living good lives. Gods of our fathers, gods of our children, gods of ourselves.

When Frances and I were married for the second time, I thought that we were mating for life. Orphaned souls, divided by war, united again. Two swans gliding together on a placid pond.

I went across town to work for the nuns of Sacré Coeur. It was Dr. Archibald who pushed me out the door. Room for only one set of hands on the levers of power.

> *We all know what will happen, said one of the men.*
> *A man is coming down the road from Jericho.*
> *Each of us must decide what he will do.*

Making public speeches. Whenever I am asked. Good evening, Gentlemen. Thanks for the invite. I never refuse an offer of pheasant and wine. Ease back in your comfortable chairs and give me a listen. Sip your after-dinner drinks and lend me your ears. John Doe was discharged from a sanitarium. Before he died he infected his wife and children, all of whom eventually died from his disease. The disease is tuberculosis. The deaths, my friends, are a crime. Who is responsible for these deaths? Let me give you a list. The family – their grandmother had been sick for twenty years, an active carrier of disease. The landlord

– the family lived in a dirty apartment, a breeder of tuberculosis germs. The first doctor – for relying on a stethoscope. The second doctor – for not examining the whole family. The sanatorium – for letting John Doe leave too soon. The government – for allowing this to happen – for letting disease be an everyday scourge in our lives. All of us are guilty. Please note that I include myself. I am part of my society, as are we all. Everything that happened was preventable. It happened here in Montréal. In the community where I live. I am devoting my life to eradicate this disease.

"A small group of social activists has prepared a paper on the desirability of introducing socialized medicine to the Province of Quebec. They are hoping to influence voters and politicians in the next Quebec Provincial Election. The chief spokesman for the group is the noted surgeon, Dr. Norman Bethune."

Catching the early-morning train for the ski-slopes.
Reading about the wars in China and Spain.

A hand attempting to squeeze a lump of coal.
God with a set of calipers making a world.
A group of people napping on a train.

He takes the paintbrush in his hand, late at night. Some pots of paint left over from the afternoon. Told the others I'd clean them up, but I let them sit there next to the sink while I read and thought. *The shattered Spanish mountain tops.* I use the same pots of paint that the kids all use. Why don't I paint the same kinds of pictures? Do I know what the kids don't know? Do I feel what the kids don't feel? *The blood bespattered faces of the dead.* Actually, the kids are smarter than we are. The kids can sense what the adults feel. They know that the world is coming at them with the speed of light. They know they'll all be here when we are all gone. *Comrades, who fought for freedom and the future world.* He dips his paintbrush in a can and draws a line.

The locked gates of a pulp and paper mill.
New unsold cars sitting on lots.
The growth of the Communist Party in Canada.

He is a man with a great disdain for familiar pathways.
He is always casting about for new ideas.

A voice in a dream - a bitter dish for me - no crystal ball - blessed by the gods - vulnerable chinks in his armour - a way of playing possum - extract my own blood - alive on the stretcher; dead on delivery - the benefit of herbs - this cold, clear mountain stream.

The poor would come to me; I didn't invite them. They would hear that I was a doctor and come to me. These were people without a dime who had nothing to give.

Keep the agony alive and you'll make a fortune. Smile like Satan when you find a disease that will make you rich. Learn to probe the patient for gold with your stethoscope.

Why is medicine marketed like cake? Why is good health reserved for the rich? Why is the commodity of compassion in such short supply?

A voice spoke to the doctor in a dream.
Physician, heal thyself! the voice repeated.
Oh, I can do that, the doctor replied.
I shall increase the size of my waiting room.

A last letter to Frances. She is marrying someone else. What to say? What to say? The best thing I can do is to set you free. I tried to make you into me; you tried to make me into you. Do you know that they x-ray Siamese twins? Before they cut them apart, I mean. What if the two of them share one heart? Or share one mind? There is a spiritual bond between us. Your new husband will walk beside you, but will not be a part of your life. I will no longer walk beside you, but my hand will be in your hand. There are people and there are ideas. You have been one and not the other to me. I imagined you, but you did not imagine me. We fail as people; we succeed as ideas. From now on, I will think of our life together as an unrealized dream. I respect the fact that you left me. You will flower if I leave you alone. Let us bring our life together to a close.

The carpenter nods towards the door of the hut.

A man searching the faces of a crowd.
A boat tugging at its anchor in a cove.
Bloody stretchers waiting to be washed.

He brushes some shavings from his piece of wood.

Words of wisdom in ancient China. Observation, auscultation and olfaction, interrogation, pulse, and palpation. These are the ways by which we diagnose.

The visitor opens the door and peers inside.

Is life a constant shedding of baggage?
Stripping our essences down to the core?

Do we leave a trail of litter as we mountain-climb?

Meeting in my apartment. Drinks all round the table. Writing a manifesto. In time for the provincial election in Quebec. A discussion paper for everyone. Citizens, doctors, politicians. *State responsibility – maintenance of the people's health – to serve the patient and the physician – preventive medicine – economic crisis of medicine – put forward a definite plan – moral responsibility – the welfare of its citizens – prime duty of the state – exploitation of the medical profession – antiquated system of fee-for-service – depression and unemployment – physical, psychiatric, racial, sociological, occupational – cure of disease for the entire population.* The Montreal Group for the Security of the People's Health. Circulated to every candidate in the coming election. How can they fail to see the logic of the truth?

Chapter 5

Canada 5

The falling-out with Archibald. For sure I lost a gamble. Had to amputate the leg. At the meeting, I admitted to every mistake. But to only operate on the safe ones, on which a surgeon takes no risks? That's not for me. Life, to me, is more like a battlefield. It goes back to my time in the War. Take the risks and accept the consequences. Nothing new will be done by surgeons in Montréal. Nothing good will be done by me if I stay where I am.

The centre of the world is wherever I am.

Two doctors arguing in a meeting.
War sitting alone with a drink in a tavern.
Mounted police charging a demonstration.

It is the place from which the ripples emanate.

A Bantu mother soothes her ailing child. The eyes are cloudy and the young girl tosses in pain. Her father has gone to fetch the medicine man.

The secret is to dive all the way down.

Is it others or is it you?
Why do your hopes so often fail?
Would you be another person in another place?

Speaking to doctors – a waste of time. For every doctor who wants changes, there are a hundred who want to sit tight. Let's just ride out this Depression and see how things go. Sure our patients have no money, but this Depression can't go on. You want the government to run the health service. It won't be long before people can pay. I want the freedom to set my own fees. We will have given up control and then where will we be?

"Police arrested speakers in Regina who wanted to address the crowd concerning the economic plight of the jobless."

"The rich will do anything for the poor but get off their backs."

Skiing can certainly have its rewards, but you have to seek them out. To travel at optimum times of the year and to seek out the finest resorts is the best way to go.

Two old doctors in a faded painting in the hospital waiting-room. Or maybe a pair of statues in the quadrangle, cast in bronze. Grey hair, furrowed brows, solemn beards. "That little girl's right lung is in a state of abscess. It would be a pretty chancy operation – to remove the lung of a ten year-old child. The new young fellow wants to try it, but I keep telling him 'no'." One bronze head leans in toward the other. Frosty breath from the lips of a statue. "Well, I sure wouldn't want to chance it. I can agree with you on that. So many things can go wrong in cases like these. Better to resign oneself to the living of life as it is." A thumb in the pocket of his waist-coat. An exhalation of frosty breath. "I'll tell the little girl's parents that there's nothing we can do." Another cold day for the statues in the quad.

The bottom falling out of the market for wheat.
Breakfast and an escort out of town.
A voucher for meat and vegetables – seventy cents.

"Bethune is delighted by the clash of minds. I can see why so many people find him attractive."
"Dr. Bethune is a man who feels thwarted. Dr. Bethune is a very bitter man."

Plunging over the edge - a poultice to soothe - many shades of ink - a very considerable strain - blood-drenched stretchers - physician heal thyself - toe to toe with the commanders - bullets, bombs and disease - the scars of the war - the edge of the slope.

What is this world that is so raw and so bleeding? What is this world that is so thriving and so green? What is my personal contribution going to be?

Religion is the marrow in my bones. Not the surface of religion, but the core. "Love thy neighbour as thyself; do onto others as you would have them do unto you."

Reaching out and flapping my wings. Testing the buoyancy of the up-draft. An eagle rising from the nest and soaring away.

The great god went for a walk.
His eyes scoured the earth from stem to stern.
All I can see are misery, carnage and pain.

Socialized medicine – a million miles away. On Mars before it ever happens here. Do you realize you're talking Socialism? Or Communism? Or worse? The politicians don't dare to lead. They want to sit back in their easy chairs and watch the wind. When the wind changes, they'll get up and lead the charge. In the meantime, all of the leading has to be done by a minuscule few.

"The Royal Canadian Mounted Police and local police in Vancouver cleared protesters out of the downtown streets using tear gas bombs."

Operating on a ten year-old child.
Drawing air from the cavity around my lung.

A man standing at the centre of the world.
A dime on a table in a cold room.
A man and a woman exchanging ideas in a coffee shop.

Montréal. St. Lawrence Boulevard at Craig Street. A line of mounted horsemen moving slowly. A crowd of demonstrators backing slowly away. "Milk for our children! Bread for our tables! We need jobs!" Helmets, shields, truncheons. The horses tugging at the reins, eager to charge. An occasional demonstrator trips and falls. Shoulder-flashes on the riders read "Police – Montreal". A bullhorn crackles loudly. "Disperse quietly to your homes and no one will be hurt! This demonstration is being conducted without a permit! Return to your homes!" The horses break into a trot. Someone falls. A rock is thrown. A whistle unleashes the power of the law. Truncheons, handcuffs, paddy-wagons. Bricks, rocks, blood. St. Lawrence Boulevard in Montreal.

Men sleeping under newspapers in the parks.
Wooden tables and porridge, soup or stew.
Seven dollars a week for a family's food.

He is a man for whom adversity is a spur to change.
He re-examines every tenet by which he lives.

Pursued by swarms of bats - the ink will not flow - a pair of mocking eyes - a kerosene lamp on a tree - if life were fair - the brutal march on the city - huddled in the rain - break the moulds - a chronic cough - the children of his being.

A piece of shrapnel caught my left leg, below the knee. Sent home to convalesce and think things over. A slight gimp in my leg and in my thoughts for the rest of my life.

I left the artsy crowd behind when I left Paris. A sense of emptiness every time I filled my glass. All they did was drink and talk in Parisian cafés.

Falling in love with Frances. Our honeymoon in Europe. Money flying out of our pockets in the wake of our skis.

The leader continued his oration to the troops.
We shall bomb their ships and tanks and planes.
We must do this for the cause.
It is essential to achieve our victory.

I'm getting weary of going to meetings. Meetings, meetings, meetings. My enthusiasm has sagged like a tired balloon. A dozen of us around a table. Hours and hours over every paragraph. Should this be a comma or a semi-colon? Is this a phrase or is this a clause? The provincial election stifled the question of public health. We spent months and months on that document. Was it used to wrap the fish or just thrown away? Aside from the drinks and the laughs, a waste of time.

An old medieval illuminated manuscript. A child in the woods. Wild and weird animals lurk behind the trees or fly overhead. A spotted tiger. A knight in shining armour. A long bright sword. A dragon is slain.

Frances has always fled to prison. To her relatives, to her second husband, to life alone. I kept my promise that she would never be bored by me.

Are you exploited or do you exploit?
How can justice be so blind?
Will you ever manage to get your thumb on the scale?

How can I look a patient in the eye and ask for money? It goes against the Hippocratic Oath. Family of five. Holes in the shoes. Patches on the pants. Faded dresses. Children shy. Clutching the skirts of the mother and holding the father's hand. Is the dime on the table theirs or is it mine? They need food; they need shelter; some crumbs on the plate and some coals in the stove. I need paintings, fine wines and a roadster. Each of us eyeing the table and wondering who gets the dime.

"In Toronto, police dispersed fifteen thousand demonstrators who were protesting the injustices of the economy."

"Our duty is to hold ourselves responsible to the people."

Fish wrapped in paper in a garbage can.
Two workers talking and laughing in a lobby.
A knight riding through sun and wind and rain.

He finds himself on a dark street. A little too much to drink. An argument with a cousin which went nowhere. Now to find his car and drive himself home. *His mental conflict so plain to read.* Not quite sure what he has encountered. What is lurking in the shadows beyond that bush? *The advance, the doubt, the retreat, the reappearance.* Slowly he advances towards it. The snow crunching like diamonds under his feet. *Suddenly crouching down on all fours.* It is late, the street is deserted, only he and the shadow are out this late at night. *The man-dog of canine mythology.* The shadow is hard to locate. Now where did he leave his car? He parked it around here somewhere. He searches in his pockets for the key.

A family on the sidewalk with all their belongings.
Work camps for single homeless men.
Women lining up for hours for a food voucher.

"Bethune is a man in whom action follows thought with great rapidity. That is his glory and his greatest source of weakness."
"Bethune is a man who is always searching. When he commits himself to something it is all-or-none."

According to his abilities - what have you done - chased by a swarm of bats - a non-aggression pact - rock beneath my feet - the opposite effect - rifles, swords and spears - the demon in me - shifting beneath his feet - the torn half-kerchief.

The gods don't need to be worshipped. They have turned their backs on us. Up to us whether we perish or survive.

When Frances and I divorced for the second time, it seemed like a part of me was gone that could not be replaced. It was me saying goodbye, at the door, to one of my selves. A bitter wind; encroaching ice; a single swan.

The nuns were devoted to people other than themselves. Not one was building a practice or nursing a career. I learned a lesson from the nuns of the Sacré Coeur.

Let us put out food at night, said one of the people.
If the wolf is well fed, he will leave us safe in our beds.
Everyone agreed to offer a sacrifice.

My trip to Russia. The USSR. Tuberculosis treatment. From the patient, not a dime. Neither class, nor means, nor income will prevent the best of care. Routine checks for tuberculosis. Disease reduced by fifty percent. Fear of communism? Fear of disorder? Fear of anarchy in the streets? Violent revolution? Civil war? A whole new order? A country giving birth. Blood and torment. Agonizing pain. Bloody mucus smears the birth of every child. Oh the fear is real all right. I can see it in your eyes. Fear of kindness. Fear of compassion. Fear of hope.

"A Royal Commission has concluded that the Federal Government and the Royal Canadian Mounted Police are blameless in the civil riot that occurred in Saskatchewan and that the rioting was incited by Communist agents."

Drinking whiskey as I watch the children paint.
Giving Marion the portrait I made of my late-night self.

An eagle rising upwards from a nest.
Ripples expanding outward on a pond.
A person living his life on a battlefield.

He parks his car along the bank and watches the river. This ice will all be ocean-bound in the spring. This will be my last jaunt in the roadster. In a few minutes, I'd better be taking her back to town. *Enough of speech; enough of thought; enough of ideas.* Been to the bank; been to the landlord; been to the lawyer. *From now on, all my thoughts will be expressed as actions.* "All my money and my goods to Frances Coleman." Hard to think of her as answering to such a name. *So many things to be done in this world.* Set aside enough to finance the Children's Art Centre. What remains of the ashes – every book, every painting, every dime – I leave to Frances. Let everything else evaporate when I'm gone.

Living on scraps of food for days at a time.
Food, lodging and twenty cents a day.
Six children, like sardines, in one bed.

He is a man whom one cannot back into a corner.
He is a cat for whom each death is a stage in his life.

Holding the future of china - people crying out in terror - a plague of grasshoppers - how best to serve - the only communication - the eyes of someone else - the value of the plan - what are the secrets - smashed into fragments - a man like me.

So there were patients without a dime who needed a doctor. And there were doctors without a dime who needed to serve. How to put two and two together and come up with four?

Hang more diplomas on your wall than the healers in heaven. Park your roadster in front of the hovels and hold out your hand. Bury your patients in unmarked graves on your way to the bank.

Is this a society without a conscience? Is this a society without a soul? Is the best response simply to leave and close the door?

Those scales would serve you well to measure silver.
Those scales would serve you well to measure gold.

Children painting on the floor of my apartment. Brushes, sheets of paper, cans of paint. Pictures of trees and clouds and sunshine. Pictures of faces, dirty or clean. Pictures of buildings looking like canyons. How much am I needed here? I pay the rent and welcome the children. I watch them paint while I fume and drink. What kind of world is waiting outside? The children paint while the adults whisper of war in Spain. Is that a scratching sound I hear? All eyes turn to the door. Better clutch your drinks and pray. Do these children have any idea what lurks outside?

A man cramming his things into a small leather bag.

At the end of it all with Frances. Twice-married & twice-divorced. Time to move on. Why such conflict between two people? Why such love since the conflict began? If she had been more like me? If I had been more like her? At what level are we one and will always be? At what level will Norman and Frances never see peace?

The water collects in a series of pools.

A doctor increasing the size of his waiting room.
An instrument which measures the depth of the soul.
A woman giving birth to a blood-smeared child.

A group of women approaches from the village.

Robes ruffle as the wind blows in off the desert. A display of Hebrew medical instruments. Scalpels, forceps, probes, needles, catheters, gynecological specula.

They throw their bundles down and fall to their knees.

Big fish in a little pond?
Every bullfrog knows who you are?
Ever consider there might be a bigger pond elsewhere?

I don't know why you were born in Canada. There's nothing happening here. Career in shreds; marriage in tatters; too rich to starve and too poor to enjoy. Reading books and discussing ideas. Waiving your fees each time you look agony square in the face. Sitting and painting in your apartment after the children have all gone home. Drawing up health-plans that no one in government bothers to read. Speaking to doctors who listen politely and then yawn and shake their heads. The medical profession barricading the door. The world in turmoil across the Atlantic. People willing to die for a cause. The war of the worlds now being fought by the peasants in Spain.

Chapter 6

Spain 1

Madrid is under siege. Franco is expecting to enter the city at any moment. A rumour is going round that he has telephoned ahead to a hotel dining room and reserved a table for tonight for his entourage. A café in our hotel. A constant babble in many tongues. Everyone is armed. Not knowing any Spanish. Knowing only English and French. Better shave off that moustache, son. They're on the look-out for Fascist spies. Your civilian clothes and your moustache will get you done in. Sorrenson arrives from Montreal. A Spanish-speaking Canadian. This will break the language barrier. We raise our glasses and clink them together. Bethune, Sorrenson, Sise. A Canadian contingent. Dodging bombs in Madrid cafés. Both of them asking me – so what do we do?

A shell bursting with a great roar nearby.

A star on the peak of a mountain.
A person breaking a mould with a hammer.
A milk bottle filled with blood.

Poor huddled bodies of rags and blood.

Preparing for surgery in the shadow of the Parthenon. The patient drifts into a dreamlike state. The family prays to the healing-god Asclepius, just in case.

Sightless eyes turned to a cruel and indifferent sky.

A battle of inches in a world-wide field?
An ant with a hazel-nut to crack?
Starting to climb a mountain that reaches as far as the clouds?

Touring the hospitals here in Madrid. Rooms filled with wounded and convalescents. An old fellow mopping up blood in the hall. Would you like to work at the International Brigades training centre in Albacete? There is an urgent need to train more medical staff. Would you like to join the medical staff of one of the military hospitals here in Madrid? We have converted our luxury hotels. We have commandeered both the Prado and the Ritz. Great praise for Spanish medicine; no curiosity about the way things are done in Canada. Breaking off the tour. Taking the others aside. I couldn't work with Spanish doctors. Jealous of foreign doctors. I can see it in their eyes. I am Canadian. I work alone. We are a unit – these others and I. We will find our own way to contribute. Gracias, gracias, gracias. What you are doing here is certainly admirable. We will find our own way out. Thanks for your time.

"Fighting continues today against the forces which seek to overthrow the legitimately-elected democratic government of Spain."

"Do unto others as you would have them do unto you."

The mountains of Spain. The Guadarramas. I borrowed skis from the ski patrol. That was the only time I got to ski in Spain.

He can barely see through the windshield. The truck grinds up the mountain pass. No sight of the trucks that were running ahead. "My God, this fog is heavy. Pea soup or cotton batten or something like that. We're supposed to turn right here somewhere, but there's nothing to see. They should have someone out on the road to help us out." He hears a shout and stops the truck. The headlights show the fog. A soldier with a rifle in his hand. "I think we're here." Another soldier in the headlights. They slowly approach the truck. "Oh my God! Look at the helmets! Fascist troops! Raise your hands! We should have taken a turn back there. A whole bloody load of ammunition. Delivered right into their hands!" The Fascist soldiers point their rifles and circle the truck. "If we don't get shot, we'll both be prisoners for the rest of the war."

Refugees struggling along a dusty road.
A soldier with a perforated intestine.
The crew of a downed aircraft laid in the sand.

"Bethune sees the living of life as a great adventure. He says that one's greatest task is to live life well."

"Dr. Bethune is my reason for coming to Spain. That such a well-established person could give it all up and come here is an inspiration to me."

A lump of coal - the sabre-toothed tiger - an organization like a globe - women, children, grandfathers - fish in a pool - posting a poem on a wall - his bread and his wine - the peak of a mountain - a drawing in great detail - the fuel which makes it glow.

I washed my hands of Canada. What else was there to do? Shook off the dust of my home and native land.

When I met Marion, it was as if we were talking through glass. I was like a prisoner in contact with the outside world. I came to know what it would be like when I got outside.

Amazing how easy it is to just walk away. Marriage dead; career in splints; Canada moribund. Spain alive but bleeding to death on a stretcher.

A man and dog out walking in the woods.
I am the better leader thinks the dog.
The better eyes, the better ears, the better nose.

Two days at the Front with the International Brigade. Visiting the trenches. Trying to find out what medical help the Front-line soldiers need. Turning down the offer of a helmet. Only a few have one to wear. How could I look myself in the eye if I accepted? Talking to the men as we keep our heads down in our collars. The occasional bullet whizzes over-top. What has been best in the medical treatment? What has been worst? What do you fear most if you were to suffer a wound? It all reminds me of 1915. There have been very few advances since the War. Men being wounded in the trenches and dying before they can be treated behind the lines. Only those who are going to survive are ever saved; those who need immediate attention are doomed to die. How to keep myself Canadian? How to remain independent of those whose incompetence will gradually drag me down? I need to develop a definite proposal or I will simply have to go into an existing hospital as just another surgeon and disappear into the crowd. I sense that the Spanish would gladly comply; those back home would soon acquiesce. I need to come up with a good idea. England has the English Hospital. Scotland has the Scottish Ambulance. Money comes to me from Canada. What can I do with Canadian money to help the cause? What can I do that will be Canadian through and through?

"The revolt of the army garrisons was quickly put down by the legitimate government in the Spanish towns of Madrid, Valencia, Albacete, Bilbao and Barcelona."

Dodging bombs in Madrid cafés.
Visiting Spanish hospitals.

A man looking through a pane of glass.
A man walking along the road from Jericho.
A person testing the sharpness of a knife.

The stretcher-bearers crouch as low as they can and still walk. Puffs of smoke drift on the crisp morning air. The wounded soldier gurgles on the stretcher. He leans way over to the side and tries to spit. The blood runs down his cheek and pools on the canvas. He thinks of his mother. He thinks of his wife. He thinks of his daughter, home on the farm. Things started out pretty good. A night in the trenches, a quick bite to eat, coffee, piping hot, and over the top. I wonder if I'll ever walk again. How could I farm if I have to use crutches? It doesn't look good. Jostled by the roughness of the terrain. Guns boom, rifles crack, machine guns bark. Someone else will get my rifle. Maybe the bullets are still in my belt. The fight will go on. The blood drips out on the stretcher. Jouncing along. Jouncing along. Jouncing along.

Children's bodies removed from shattered houses.
A German soldier with a massive wound in his thigh,
Sceptical doctors discussing a blood transfusion plan.

He is a man who takes an x-ray of all he encounters.
He is a man who re-invents the conditions of life.

Six cents per person per day - blinded in one of his eyes - a mind which is on fire - darkness in the village - sleeping in a cave - of course I am the leader - a calmness of spirit - need to know - operate without anaesthetics - everything else is nothing.

Spain was a dying, bleeding corpse. The Fascist jackals were having a feast. How could a doctor read the news and not go to Spain?

I saw it in the trenches in 1915. Stretchers leaned against the walls soaked in blood. Men would die for no other reason than lack of blood.

Sorensen, Sise, May – "The Three Amigos". "Norman Bethune and His Band of Merry Men". "The Blood Brothers" I used to call us, when I'd had a few drinks.

You drill three holes in the cranium the physician told his assistant.
The aim is to relieve the pressure inside the skull.
This technique has come down from ancient lore.

A blood-transfusion unit! That's what will keep the wounded alive! Not the one that the Spanish already have. Its headquarters are in Barcelona. Any soldier who lives long enough to survive the journey from the scene of a battle to the blood-transfusion unit in Barcelona will be saved, of course, but anyone who needs blood on the battlefield will surely die. Explaining my thoughts to Sorensen. Guess what! The blood will be delivered! This is the new idea! The blood will be delivered to the Front! Demand and supply. What is the link between these two? The link will be the storage and the transportation of the blood! Battles are raging near Madrid! We ask the population of Madrid to do their part in defeating the Fascists by donating blood! We stabilize the blood! We transport it to the Front on the eve of a battle! A militiaman is wounded, the stretcher-bearers bring him to us and we give him blood! Sorensen! Stop reading that drivel and listen! The whole idea is so simple it cries out for life!

A young man and a girl. A ditch between the two. The young man urges her to jump. The girl hesitates. Whether to jump or whether to bide? She is distracted by a story that she has heard.

Her second husband was the stone, grey walls of the dungeon. She fled into a prison to escape from me. Unlike Frances, when I move on, I seek to be free.

Why so hard on the Spanish doctors?
Are they not trying to do their best?
Do you see them as your rivals for fame and prestige?

Making a proposal to the Socorro Rojo International in Valencia. Laying out my plans. We will take the blood to the Front! Every death that does not happen instantly on the field of war is a preventable death! The secret will be in the stabilization of the blood! Good work in being done by the Spanish Blood-transfusion unit, but it is anchored to the ground in Barcelona! My plan will save the ones they cannot save! We have come a long way since the War! There are many new techniques! It is no longer 1915! All the money will come from Canada. It will be a great boost to fund-raising. It is important that it be independent and have a title which makes it known as Canadian. Writing to the Committee to Aid Spanish Democracy in Toronto. Asking for permission to proceed as planned. The Scots and English have their field hospitals. We will have our mobile blood-transfusion service. It will be called the *Servico Canadianse de Transfusion de Sangre*. You send the money and I will save the lives.

"In many Spanish towns, the ill-equipped workers and peasants seem to be overcoming the better-equipped but small army garrisons and are handing the Fascist rebels what many observers hope is a stunning defeat."

"The only antidote to mental suffering is physical pain."

A dog asleep outside a lighted window.
A man changing clothes and shaving off his moustache.
People looking like black ants on a street.

The doctor leans over his patient. The body of a child. Stretched out on the operating table. Rescued from the ruins of a bombed-out building. *How beautiful the body; how perfect its parts; with what precision it moves.* This boy must be five or six. Was it a house or was it a store? Was anyone brought in with him? *How obedient, proud and strong.* Wonder if his parents are still alive. People get buried in the ruins. You can hear their cries, sometimes, but they can't be reached. *How terrible when torn; the little flame of life sinks lower, flickering quietly and gently.* Check the anaesthetic, another scalpel, we'll need more blood in a minute. He's not lost yet. *It makes its protest against extinction, a candle clinging to the last of life, and then goes out.* Between air-raids the other day, I saw a mother buying a tricycle in a shop.

A truck-load of food and blankets for refugees.
A bullet still inside a shoulder eluding a probe.
Three children lying dead on the cobblestones.

"Bethune has cut his ties with Canada. He seems to feel that the country has let him down."
"Bethune is a man who believes in international brotherhood. He would like to see everyone in the world holding hands."

Accept the consequences - as a fish swims - the soldiers who need us most - deeper into the woods - you must follow me - the eyes of someone else - a slope of sparkling snow - the calipers in my hand - the loss of so many patients - the music of you.

The Spanish doctors were hard to figure out. I hired some of them to work with the Canadian team. They resented having to take their orders from me.
It was easy to understand Hitler. Mussolini's motives were clear. It was everyone else in this mess that I wondered about.

The Communists in Spain had the purest motives. They were the ones who felt their brotherhood with Spain. They wanted nothing but that the Spanish people be free.

A light shone on the peak of a mountain.
A peasant climbed to the top.
When he got there, he found a star.
He left it there and went to dwell in the valley below.

Shopping in London. Sorensen and I. Can't get what we want in Paris. A Ford station car. 1½ tons of cargo. One hundred and seventy-five pounds Stirling. Alterations to the luggage rack. Built-in boxes. Independent of electrical power. Refrigerator powered by kerosene. Auto clave by gasolene. Sterilization of solutions and bottles and such. Incubator by kerosene. Distilled water-still by kerosene. One hundred and seventy-five pieces of glassware. Vacuum bottles, blood flasks, drip bottles, containers. Froud syringes, microscope haemocytometers, chest instruments, type 2 and 3 blood serum for testing blood groups. Hurricane lamps, gas masks, chemicals to make up solutions for intravenous injections of physiological serums, glucose and sodium citrate for three months. All packed in water-tight cases.

"It is said that, from his stronghold in the Spanish colony of Morocco, Generalissimo Francisco Franco is plotting his next move."

Writing poetry during the night.
Going to London to buy a truck.

A man who sees through another's eyes.
A person washing his hands.
A great god going for a walk.

He can't sleep. Restless thoughts run through his mind. He rolls over and plumps up the pillow. The words of a poem run through his mind. *My eyes are overflowing and clouded with blood.* The window is open and a siren calls out in the night. *The blood of a young woman. The blood of a very old man. The blood of many people.* A sliver of moonlight on the clock. He has set the alarm. *Cubs of a man-eating wolf.* Morning will come early. *Blood of brothel and mud.* He gets up and scribbles some words. He lies down on his cot and rolls over and tries to sleep.

Blood treated with sodium citrate to prevent coagulation.
Three fighter-planes attacking two small bombers.
A sobbing woman holding a broken child.

He is a man for whom adversity is an invitation.
There is no mountain which is too high for him to climb.

A flimsy hollywood set - slowly bleeding to death - a wolf gobbling lambs - a new lease on life - given up control - a restless soul - the crooked diploma - an extra child - to ensure his care - a great sense of responsibility.

There is a knife that's still buried in my back. A knife that was forged in Canada and wielded in Spain. With the finger-prints of Sorensen, Sise and May.

The orphanage was the greatest blow of them all. A million homeless kids all over Spain. I brooded and brooded and finally figured out what to do.

What to say about what happened in Spain? I search my brain to find the words. I find none.

In the beginning, I made a world, said God.
I made it with the calipers in my hand.
I said let there be light and there was light.
Everything I made, I made of chaos;
There is chaos in everything I made.

Driving through Paris and down to Madrid. Flocks of geese and yokes of oxen. Explaining my project to Sorensen as we make our way. We will appeal through the press and radio for daily donations. Eight hundred or a thousand donors would be good to start. We will group their blood and make a card-index file. Fifty-six hospitals in Madrid. We make a survey of their needs: size, capacity, address, organization, telephone, chief surgeon, type of service. We have a map of the city and our routes. We collect from our list of donors, every day, for groups I, II, III, and IV. A gallon a day from each. Store it in our refrigerator. Phone call from the hospital. Transfer blood to vacuum flask. Bottle of warm physiological serum and glucose solution, sterilized tin box with towel, forceps, knife, syringe, catgut, group testing serum. Best have fifteen sets of these. On arrival at a site, we will start to work. My pencil scrawls as Sorensen hits a pot-hole. Shade and sunlight dance on my paper. Important that I make sure to get everything down.

A light in the dyer's window.

A man walking his donkey along a road.
A group of people crouching down in a patch of grass.
The only person who is living in the world.

The dyer's dog asleep outside.

Roman engineers with plans for building an aqueduct. Clean water from the hills. A sewage system to curb the incidence of disease.

No one comes and goes at this hour of the night.

Are your ducks moving into a line?
Is this, finally, what you were born to do?
Your best-self and your worst-self in a war-time truce?

A fifteen-room flat in Madrid. Just below the Socorro Rojo Internacionale head offices. A big old Fascist palace with plenty of room. *Servicio Canadiense de Transfusion de Sangre* painted on the side of the mobile unit. I have made myself the Director. Sorensen – Liaison Officer. Sise – Driver and General Utility Man. Two Spanish medical students. A Spanish biologist. Technician – Mrs. Celia Greenspan. Four servants, a cook, two maids and a laundry man. Armed guards at our door. Madrid is at the Front. One quarter of Madrid has been damaged. Three hundred thousand have been evacuated – mostly women and children. Seven or eight thousand killed by bombardment so far. Bombed by German Junkers yesterday. Shortage of water but no epidemics as yet. No coal, no meat, no butter, no sugar. Plenty of vegetables and fruit. Franco is massing troops and materials near the city. He says he will not leave one stone standing in Madrid. Morale is good among the people. I am here and I am ready to start my work.

Chapter 7

Spain 2

Bombs are falling in Madrid. They started to fall at noon. Twelve Italian tri-motor bombers droning slowly overhead. Not looking for military targets. Looking for the poorest parts of town. People living in one and two-storey mud and brick houses. Mainly women, children and old people. The young men are all fighting at the Front. It is war against civilians! They want panic in the city! Standing in a doorway. Glancing up and down the street. A hush over the city. People shuffling to refugios. Hunted animals crouched in the grass. There is no escape.

A great leviathan racing upward from the deep.

People huddled in doorways.
A black horse contentedly munching a bag of oats.
A castle at the top of a rocky cliff.

Viewing the world of men with an all-embracing eye.

A Vaidya speaking to his followers in ancient India. The art of healing has always been treated with respect. For generations we have passed this knowledge down.

Plunging back down into the depths to give new birth.

Do you think while bombs are dropping?
Are you oblivious while tending a wound?
If you thought at any depth would it drive you insane?

The death ships pause and drop their cargo. Huge bombs tear through the roofs. Through every floor of the buildings. Exploding in the basements. Bringing down the wood and the concrete. Pulling everything down inside. Doorways are better than basements. Falling brick and wood and stone. The bombs descending like great black pears. Thunderous roars when they hit their targets. They want fear in all the hearts! They want us terrified! Heaps of huddled clothes on the sidewalks and the streets. Blood flowing into the gutters and settling in pools. Cries of the wounded and the buried alive. Sirens of ambulances. Roars of flames. Blackened and crumpled bodies. Working with the wounded all day in the streets. Finally settling down and getting some sleep.

"The leader of the forces which seek to overthrow the legitimately-elected democratic government of Spain is Generalissimo Francisco Franco."

"Capital is reckless of the health or length of life of the labourer, unless under compulsion from society."

A thick covering of fresh snow, bright sunshine and a stunning mountain view. Sitting on the patio and sipping hot chocolate with friends. Pity the person who never learns to ski.

He sits in a circle of soldiers. Silhouettes and a sliver of moon. No risk of a campfire tonight. "If they capture you, they will kill you." Hoping his ancient rifle won't jamb. "They will line you up with the others, maybe a fence or against a wall. They will have a firing squad or maybe a machine gun. The first thing they do is kill all the males. That way you can't come back to haunt them. That's the way they think. Then the women – well, what can I say? The women will have to fend for themselves. If only half the rumours are true, then it's a bad, bad thing if a woman is taken alive. It's a lot easier being a man, that's for sure. If you're wounded, they'll put you to death – with a bullet or a bayonet – and that'll be that."

Smoke trailing from the engine of a bomber.
An ariel bombardment continuing day after day.
A plate of olive oil and Spanish beans.

"Dr. Bethune is seen by many as lacking in discipline. He has an inborn inability to suffer fools."

"Bethune is a man in love with the smell of danger. He waves his sword and plunges straight ahead."

Name, battalion, wound, date of receipt - the peak of a mountain - see what I cannot see - two doctors arguing - the brains boil - a slab of honey - an offer of pheasant and wine - living in biblical times - another cold day - walking around the world.

When I was young, I saw it all differently. I saw Canada and myself as two friendly equals. I owed Canada just exactly what she owed me.

Marion was a socialist. Marion was an artist. Marion was a very compassionate soul.

I presented myself to the Canadian Red Cross. Volunteered to join their medical expedition. The Red Cross had no plans for service in Spain.

Young Proffit confronted the two workers.
Eenie, meenie, minie, moe, he chanted.
Then he glared at the worker at the end of his finger and snapped, You're
fired!

The mobile blood-transfusion unit. Middle of the night. A phone call for blood. They've got a couple of boys over at the hospital. Snatching up our packed bag. Opening the refrigerator. Two 500 cc bottles of blood. One of Group IV and one of Group II. Rousing our armed guard. Yawning and stretching and reaching for their guns. Placing our equipment in the truck. *Servicio Canadiense de Transfusion de Sangre.* All of us in as the engine grinds to life. Driving through the streets. Completely black. No streetlights and no moon. In Madrid, we are already at the Front.

"Generalissimo Franco has declared that as soon as his Fascist armies achieve victory, the Spanish Republic is to be abolished and the government of Spain will be totalitarian."

Writing to Canada for more support.
Making a list of all the hospitals in Madrid.

The steady tac-tac-tac of machine guns.
Bombs raining on ships and tanks and planes.
A doctor holding an x-ray up to the light.

He leaves the clearing station hospital and walks across the fields. The wreckage of the planes have cooled overnight. *The bodies of those men who died.* He takes the screwdriver and removes the plate from the German engine. Best way to prove that the game is not being played according to the rules. *Thousands of miles from their native lands.* An attack by fifteen German and Italian bombers. Resisted by one solitary government plane. They set him on fire but he managed to take one with him. Drove head-on into one of Franco's planes. *Under this old Spanish sun, among the vines and olive trees of this beautiful land.* Both planes crashed on a vine-covered hill, both pilots dead as they hit the ground. Both pilots removed and given a burial yesterday.

A shelf of milk bottles filled to the brim with blood.
A cup of milk and a piece of dried bread.
A package of much-needed x-ray films.

He is a man who has no patience for things as they are.
He sees life as a series of problems which he can solve.

Intellectual and spiritual life - people without a dime - water springing from a rock - first to blink - the clash of minds - signed by many hands - the eyes are cloudy - swatting pesky flies - I had the illusion - the lions' fanged maws.

A democratically-elected government. Under bombardment by a military force. Reforms by elected officials overthrown.

They would take the stretchers and rinse off the blood and use them again. Some men would live and some would die while being carried back from the Front. I could have told the stretcher-bearers which would be which.

Sorensen putting a splint on my fractured Spanish. Sise recording the pain on the Almeria road. May writing despatches back home to Canada.

Famine sat alone with his drink in a tavern.
Outside the window, his black horse munched his oats.
I have tried to starve Death but to no avail.
I need a less-formidable foe to destroy.

Machine guns chatter and then fall silent. A series of single rifle shots. The driver pauses at each crossroads and then proceeds. The grounds of the hospital. An exchange of words with the guards. Blood! We come with blood! The doctors phoned! Through the door and then the flashlight. Clumping down the stairs. All of the operating rooms have been moved to the cellars. A man lying on a stretcher. Kneeling down beside. The flashlight shows the loss of blood. Opening the bag. Sterilized box of instruments and towels. Are you okay, Amigo? He doesn't talk.

Sailing across the sea. A great ship, like a Spanish galleon. The ship comes near a rocky coast. The sirens sing their songs. They lure me off my course. I leave the ship and beauteous creatures point the way up a rocky cliff. A splendid castle at the top. I am attacked by swarms of bats. They strike me down.

I told Frances that I lend her out; I don't give her away. Her second husband has no claim on the gem in her soul. I laid claim to the deepest level and never let go.

What is the rationale of a hand-grenade?
What is the logic of a bayonet?
What are the thoughts of the hand which releases the bomb?

This boy has lost a lot of blood. Pricking the finger. Extracting a drop. Putting one drop each of Serum type II and Serum type III on the slide. Checking his red blood cells. Agglutinated by II or by type III? Is he I or III or IV? No, he's II — he'll have to have II. Too bad we can't use IV. We're running low. Warming the blood in a pan of water. Just about ready to start. Looking carefully at his face. Hard to tell in the lights we have. Deciding the face is white as a sheet. An almost imperceptible pulse. I'd say he's both shocked and exsanguinated. Injecting novocaine over the vein in the bend of the elbow.

"Franco has vowed that as soon as he is victorious, he will revoke the measures which have led to land reform and restore the estates to the large landowners."

"Communists unite with the people, take root and blossom among them."

Sirens singing a song at the edge of a cliff.
A drop of blood on a glass slide.
A man attempting to write a letter home.

The operating room at the Palace Hotel. Crystal chandeliers like an orchard heavy with glass. Gold-framed mirrors that used to glitter when revellers danced at the ball. *From every country in Europe.* Eight tables, side by side. Two doctors at each table, an anaesthetist and a nurse. *Left their wives and families.* Multiple perforations of the intestine. A soldier shot through the abdomen and left to die. *In the pride of their young strength.* An anti-fascist German soldier. Shot through the thigh with a dum-dum bullet. The exit hole as large as a clenched fist. An anti-tetanus serum and a blood transfusion. *Fighting and dying for an ideal of human freedom.* A Pole shot through the shoulder. An x-ray shows the doctor where to probe. The Palace operating room on a busy day.

Soldiers dying of shock and loss of blood.
Fascist troops entering a deserted town.
The rattle of machine guns in the dark.

"Bethune is a man of short-lived enthusiasms. He is liable to cut and run at any time."

"Bethune is a very thorough organizer. He has the blood-transfusion service ticking like a well-tuned clock."

The buoyancy of the updraft - the barrel of a gun - the language barrier - pain and fear in the eyes - he becomes all men - a fair share of the benefits - tugging at its anchor - nowhere for anyone to hide - disease as a crippling presence - a duckling or a swan.

The Spanish doctors thought of themselves as Spanish. I thought of myself as International. I thought of myself as having left Canada behind.

There were volunteers from over twenty democratic nations. They were eager to stifle Fascism at its birth in a cave. Not one of the democratic governments took part in the war.

Hitler was fighting for Spanish iron and manganese. Mussolini was fighting for Mediterranean glory. The Russians were fighting only to help their brothers in Spain.

I have decided what I will do, said the first man.
I will rob him of his money and his clothes.
I will leave him by the roadside waiting for death.

Cutting down and finding the vein and inserting a small glass Canula. Running in the blood. Always nice to see the change. This one is spectacular. Giving him 500 cc of preserved blood. Pausing to see if he'll need some more. Following up with a 5% solution of glucose. Enjoying the surging of the pulse. Watching the colour return to his lips. This boy is okay!

"The Spanish church, which is the nation's largest landowner, has thrown its support behind the forces of Franco and is urging all Christians to fight against the Republic as an act of faith."

Removing blood-stained rags from damaged legs.
Comforting children with feet swollen to twice their size.

An operating room with chandeliers.

People leaving food outside their doors.
The howls of a young child in a cave.

A hospital in Madrid. Heavy fighting today. Exhausting work. He tries to catch a couple of winks. *The steady tac-tac-tac of the machine guns.* The sound comes through the heavy shutters. The sound comes through the thick, oak door. *The gun-fire is almost continuous.* It's the clear, cold winter air. Makes it sound like the fighting is at the end of the street. *Like the Front in 1915.* The machine guns are taking up the slack. A bit of a lull until the bombers reload and return. *Brace yourself for the onslaught.* If we hear them drone, we'll be in for a busy night.

The uniting of liberals, socialists and communists.
Screaming people with their faces covered in blood.
Political correspondents at the hotel bar.

He is a man who brings light and life to all who know him.
He is a doctor who brings his patients back from the dead.

A trail of litter - everything that his father owned - a bitter lesson to learn - a balanced scale - only what he needed - transpose the reality - clothing, socks and gloves - thirsty people fail to drink - a pretty chancy operation - misery, carnage and pain.

Sorensen and I spent many hours together. We drove down together from Paris with the new mobile-unit. How could I know that he was sharpening his knife?

Build an orphanage in Spain, far up in the hills. Far from the killing; far from the blood. A refuge from the crashing sound of the guns.

How to re-construct experience? To write the simple, the moving, the true? How to write what I want the people back home to know?

A voice spoke to the doctor in a dream.
Physician, heal thyself! the voice insisted.
Oh, I can do that, the doctor replied.
I will turn away those patients who have no cash.

Early morning in Madrid. The sun comes through the windows of the hospital. A cup of coffee to welcome the day. Making sure the patients are stabilized. A French boy and a Spaniard. They both got hit quite hard. One boy was an arm and another was liver and stomach. Side by side in the Clearing Station. The French boy clenches his fist. Vive la Révolution, mon médecin! The Spanish boy waves good-bye. It is nothing, mi doctor, nada. I will fight again. A quick word with the medical staff. Call us if you need us. Never know what the day will bring.

A child in a bundle of clothing in a small bed.

A maiden staring down into lions' maws.
A line of children in a street.
The pin of a hand-grenade.

A woman bending over and wiping its nose.

Busy chatter in the marketplace in Bagdad. Exchanging lore on the curing of disease. Stomach ulcers, breast cancer, facial paralysis.

Tucking a blanket up around its neck.

What is the secret of men of action?
What do they know that the rest don't know?
Do Hitler and Mussolini think at all?

In the truck and on our way back to the centre. Picking our way among the debris. Piles of bricks and wood and plaster. Yesterday we did three transfusions. Have to appeal for more blood. Need more to leave at the hospitals. Collecting about ½ to ¾ gallon daily, mixing it with Sodium Citrate, at 3.8%, keeping it just above freezing in the refrigerator, in sterile milk or wine bottles. This keeps the blood for about a week. Locke's Solution preserves the blood longer. Bayliss's Gum Solution too. Every boy has a story to tell me. We could use more foreign nurses. Language can be a problem here in Spain.

Chapter 8

Spain 3

Evening in Almeria. A little seaport pressed against the mountains. Thousands of people who have walked here from Malaga. Many are bruised and bleeding. Shelled and fired on as they swarmed along the road. Twenty-five thousand troops invaded Malaga! There were Moors, Germans, Italians! They attacked with tanks and ships and airplanes! A line of children in the street, standing in front of an open door. A cup of milk and a handful of bread. Huddling in small groups as they eat in silence. All of them wonder if they are orphans. Most of them will have to sleep in the street.

Every life must have a purpose.

A little girl with a broken doll.
A perfect day on the slopes.
A photo of people straggling along a road.

In the light of that purpose, life becomes good and fine and free.

A drawing in great detail on papyrus. Written in hieratic script in ancient Egypt. An aid to an operation on the eye.

Against that purpose, everything else is nothing.

What is there about you that is changing?
What is there about you that has never changed at all?
What is the single note that is always the music of you?

In the operating room of the Socorro Rojo Hospital. Surgeons amputating the arm of one of the bomber-crew. We had only a small band of troops! We could not hold the city! We could only buy some time for people to flee! Giving him a blood transfusion. Watching his life slowly slipping away. The blood was from Barcelona. It might have gone bad. No, he was too far gone to save. It wasn't the blood. Perhaps you're right, but it might be that the blood was spoiled by the shaking of the Renault. All of our equipment took a beating on the Almeria Road.

"It is estimated that volunteers from as many as twenty-five nations have made their way to Spain to fight on behalf of the democratically-elected government."

"Capital is dead labour, which, vampire-like, lives only by sucking living labour."

Soft, fluffy, freshly-fallen snow. Take your ski-gloves off and savour the texture. You know you're in for a perfect day on the slopes.

A woman lying in the dust along the roadside. Twenty feet perhaps from the shuffling crowd. Her legs are sprawled and there is something in her lap. She makes no sound. There is shade from the remnant of an olive bush. It covers her shoulders and her chest but not her head. Her head is bare and there are droplets on her brow. She is suckling a child. It is covered with a dusty blanket. She wets her lips with her tongue and squints in the glare of the sun. The blanket slips down from her breast. Her hand is too tired to hold it. The child is exposed. "Water. I need water. I have no milk." She has walked all the way from Malaga. Others have helped her to carry the child. Her shoes are worn to nothing. Perhaps they were velvet or some kind of silk. She can no longer go on. She can only lie down. "Please take my child to Almeria. My husband will look for her there. Please save my child." People are walking six abreast. A column as far as the eye can see. The sun beats down. They are covered in dust. Exhaustion is a weight that pulls them down. "Is there anyone who can take an extra child?"

The steady drone of the anti-aircraft sirens.
A stable filled with wounded on the Almeria Road.

Bombers with a fighter escort returning again.

"Bethune has found himself a kingdom. He rules the blood-transfusion service as his personal fief."

"Bethune has never been a joiner. If he can't be in command, he'll walk away."

The simple human need - medicinal herbs in a garden - a sense of emptiness - your best thoughts - a red pterodactyl - a man plunging a needle - name, nationality, date of death - a million miles away - unrolling a scroll and reading - stripping our essences.

For sure there are people who break your heart. But the greatest breaker of hearts, I would say, is ideals. Canada came very close to breaking me.

Marion taught me to see. I flattered her one day. I said that I looked into her eyes and saw myself.

I saw an article in the newspaper. The formation of a Spanish Hospital and Medical Aid Committee. I presented myself in Toronto the very next day.

The great god rubbed his forehead.
My eyes are old and I cannot see as I used to do.
Perhaps a messenger can see what I cannot see.

Talking to the International Red Cross. A man named Phillips. Giving him a piece of my mind. How can you not know what's going on out there? Don't you realize how disastrous this is? Why don't you jump in your car and go see for yourself? The refugees are still pouring along the road! They knew that they would be shot or raped! They left a deserted town for the Fascists to find! One hundred and fifty-thousand! Every one of them is on this road! Phillips and Sise leave in the Red Cross car. Sending Sise with his camera and film. If the Red Cross doesn't believe it, neither will anyone else back home. A photographic record to show to the world.

"The international volunteers are entering Spain illegally, as most of the democratic governments have forbidden their citizens to fight on behalf of a foreign nation. These volunteers – students, workers, idealists and intellectuals – are being referred to as The International Brigades."

Digging for bodies in shattered mud and brick buildings.
Giving a blood transfusion to a shopper on the cobble-stone street.

A pair of scales on a mantel.
A cup of milk and a handful of bread.

A document which has been signed by many hands.

A child of ten. A little boy. Bare feet cut and bleeding. Sitting rubbing his foot at the edge of the road. Hundreds of peasants flow by in an endless stream. Where did Daddy go? He was carrying my brother and sister. I don't know where he is. Nearby, an old lady lies prone. Gigantic swollen legs. Open varicose ulcers. Battered linen sandals. The boy crouches down beside her. When will Grandma awake? When will Daddy come back? Where is everybody going? The road is sharp white flint. Nowhere to get a drink. People struggled down to the creek, but it was dry.

Newspaper appeals for the collection of blood.
Heavy fighting in the suburbs of Madrid.
The rationing of milk and bread and meat.

He is a man who has no patience with incompetence.
He is a man who has always swept the stodgy aside.

Stripping your life to the bones - bricks, rocks, blood - who gets the dime
- the logic of the truth - others first; yourself last - the healing god, alscepius -
what I wish to weigh - all four sides of the cage - a pair of statues - a crystal ball.

Rifles against machine guns. Grenades against tanks. Pitchforks fighting against the mechanized forces of war.

We were only saving the living. We were not preventing death. Hundreds and thousands were bleeding to death before they reached help.

Saving lives in the Guadarramas. Saving lives on the plains. Driving our mobile-units all over Spain.

The leader continued his oration to the troops.
We shall bomb their factories, cities and towns.
We must do this for the cause.
It is essential to achieve our victory.

Watching repairs to the mobile-unit. It wasn't built for this kind of a beating. Three days of rescuing refugees from Malaga. The mechanic checking the tires. Replacing the oil in the crankcase, checking the radiator for holes. When the morning comes, we'll go back on the road and get Sise. Thousands of refugees in the city. It is a hundred miles from Malaga to Almeria! There is only one road! There was nowhere for anyone to hide! We were trapped between the mountains and the sea!

The girl tells a story. Once there was a maiden, the girl says to her young man, who dropped her scented kerchief – down, down, down – into the enclave where the lion roared for prey. If you do not fetch my kerchief, said the maiden to the knight, you will never more find favour in my eyes.

Why would Frances leave me twice? Why would Frances claim me twice? What is the glue that binds us together and won't let go?

Would you have been a better person if you were more like Frances? Would Frances have been a better person if she were more like you? Would you both have been better if your jagged edges had matched?

Suddenly a siren. It cuts the air of the silent town. Every eye turns up to the darkness. Thirty seconds to run and hide. The battleship in the harbour? The military barracks at the edge of town? Where will the bombs fall? Are we all right here? Huddled, exhausted refugees. Massed in the centre of town. Many too tired to get up and run under a porch. Bombs from the air! Shells from the ships! We are helpless to defend ourselves! Lights flicker as the siren sounds. The ground begins to shake. Loud explosions in the air. Ducking down in the street. A shower of glass and metal and wood. Women and children and old people! They have walked for miles and miles! Their feet are bruised and swollen and covered in blood!

"The governments of Britain and France, in an effort to limit the carnage in Spain, have asked a number of nations to sign a non-intervention agreement which will ban the selling and shipping of arms to either side in the Spanish conflict. It is to be hoped that such a move will limit the amount of blood being shed on the soil of Spain."

"A revolution is not a dinner party, or writing an essay, or painting a picture, or doing embroidery."

A drawing on papyrus.
Warriors guarding the gates of a castle.
A woman slapping a cloth against a stone.

Children crying out in fear. Children seeing a crow in the distance and crying out that it's a plane. People running into the woods to get away. A little girl alone on the road with her broken doll. Her aunt and her mother are gone. They were wounded and put in a truck and driven away. Everyone ran away to the woods and left her alone. "That little girl out there! That girl has been left behind! That plane is going to dive and strafe the road!" Who was it who promised to help her? Why didn't they take her along? Everyone here is a mother or father. It makes no sense to run out on the road. Would she hear us if we shouted? Make any difference if she would lie down? Will anyone help her if she is alive when the plane is gone?

Seventy-five thousand Italian troops in Spain.
Men and girls carrying rifles in Madrid.
Noble death among the vines and olive trees.

"Bethune is a hell of a good surgeon, there is no doubt of that. He is fast and brilliant, though he occasionally makes mistakes."

"Bethune is thought of as brash and pushy. Most of the doctors see him as someone who doesn't fit in."

A spur to change - a rocky cliff - a modern priestly craft - a comma or a semi-colon - an equal claim to life - all condemned to die - the man-dog of canine mythology - a child at play - as far as the clouds - the self we murder.

Relatives on the payroll. Large gaps in their medical knowledge. Emotional outbursts during surgery; autocratic and out of control.

There was a constant jockeying for position. The Democrats, the Socialists, the Republicans; the Left, the Centre, the Right. After we won, who was going to rule in Spain?

There were only two Communists in the Republican government. There were only a few thousand Communists in Spain. They had nothing to gain but the brotherhood of man.

The plan is working, said one of the people.
We can now feel safe from the wolf.
He gobbles our lambs and chickens and pigs during the night.

One by one the bombs explode. Five and six and eight and ten. Ten large bombs dropped by the German and Italian planes in the centre of town. Whole sides of buildings sag down on the street. Gas fires blaze and light the scene. People crying, people moaning, people shouting out other's names. They attacked us along the road! The airplanes attacked us as we hid in ditches! The ships used searchlights to fire their shells at night! What seems like an endless rain of bombs. All the carnage of a barrage. After the bombs stop, whole walls come tumbling down. Screams and shouts and crying. Where are you? Where did you go? Are you all right? Buildings soaring in flames. No water to put them out. People shield their faces from the heat and search for the wounded.

"The governments of Germany and Italy have signed the non-intervention pact which was proposed by Britain and France. The move is being hailed as a master-stroke in international diplomacy which will soon be seen to limit the carnage in the Spanish civil conflict."

Demanding to know why medical instruments are not being sterilized.
Miming instructions to a nurse who does not speak English or French.

Stragglers between the mountains and the sea.
A set of scales not used to measure gold.
A dry creek where thirsty people fail to drink.

Half asleep and half awake. Sorensen at the wheel. A bumpy stretch in the road. Head jostling back and forth from a lump in the tire. He adjusts his rolled-up jacket against the window. *Perhaps some day, the world will be what I want it to be.* Rolling along in a half-ton truck. Purchased in Marseilles. Driving back to Barcelona. *Perhaps some day, the world will be a place where humans can live.* Two electro box refrigerators running on one hundred and twenty-five volts each. Twenty batteries, a dynamo and a gas engine to charge the batteries. All to be installed on our return. *Sunshine, clouds, blue skies, a gentle rain.* Nice to have a chance to close the eyes. He rolls the window down in hopes of a breeze.

A tourniquet made from the wires of a downed plane.
German bombers circling lazily over Madrid.
Name, nationality, date of death.

He is a man who has always fought against injustice.
A man whom the angels know to be on their side.

A set of scales - things to be done in this world - the shadow is hard to locate - a staff in my hand - a dying, bleeding corpse - a single cent - back down into the depths - this turbulent maelstrom - one favourite book - a child in the woods.

Sise helped draw up the plans for the orphans' refuge centre. We rescued refugees together on the road to Almeria. How could I know that he was readying his knife?

Don't send the kids out of Spain. Spain is their heritage; Spain's in their blood. These kids are the future healers of the wound.

The bare bones of fact; the swollen, exaggerated shape of fantastically-coloured romanticism. One is poverty; one is excess. Both are false.

I bought those scales and put them on the mantel.
Those scales do not measure what I wish to weigh.

Pushing through the crowd. Shouting Medico! Medico! Medico! Jagged masonry, shattered timber, electrical wires. Faces covered in blood. Some of them wrapped with torn pieces of cloth. Checking the wounds of the victims to see which ones we can help. We should have stayed in Malaga! How do we know that we would have been shot? My brother walked all the way to Almeria only to die! We had no planes or soldiers to protect us! We would scramble for the ditch! The planes would fly down low and use their machine guns! Binding up the wounds. Our army fled the city! Everyone feared the Moors! Three warships appeared in the harbour! Hold that flashlight so I can see. We're going to need more donors for blood. Take these people and put them in our room in the hotel. There must be fifty who have been murdered! They were unarmed and lining up for a piece of bread! Why would they drop their bombs in the centre of the town?

A group of women perched on the rocks.

Armies attacking a deserted town.
Surgeons amputating an arm.
A person looking through another person's eyes.

The water gurgles by in a rocky gulch.

Martinus de la Cruz writing phonetic Aztec as he records the words of a healer. Water Nettle, Pine Resin, Popcorn Flower, Bloodstone. The Indian Book of Medicinal Herbs.

They slap the cloths against the stone as the water runs down.

Would you go back and try things over?
Would you want to live life again?
What is the one thing that, perhaps, you could better have done?

A droning sound and all eyes turn up to the sky. The bellies of the bombers in the light of the fires. Circling overhead to see what they've done. Preparing to drop another load of bombs. It was the German Condor Legion! They bombed the centre of town! The cruiser in the harbour they didn't touch! Only two soldiers have been killed! Why would they bomb these children? They weren't doing any harm! They were only lining up for milk and food! Three dead children lying in the street. The street light shines on them eerily. A broken cup and a pool of spilled milk. A tiny crust of bread. A small boy stoops and pops it into his mouth.

Chapter 9

Spain 4

Crossing a rickety bridge. Coming into Guadalajara. Eleven o'clock in the morning. Clear and cold and bright. Driving the Ford. Accompanied by Sorensen, Geysa and Calbras. A refrigerator and ten pint bottles of preserved blood in a wire basket. We left Madrid at ten. Fifty clicks in less than an hour. She's a pretty good road.

Un-compromise, un-contact, un-contamination.

A note which asks for help.
A man who tries to think like a dog.
A man who attempts to realize an ideal.

The cure for the constant pain in my heart.

An Assyrian doctor palpating a patient. Asking questions in an effort to find out where it hurts. Asking the wife if her husband has had these symptoms before.

The road that I must travel down alone.

Is your soul a part of your marrow?
Is it part of your muscle and bone?
Is your soul the thing that boils inside your skull?

Checking the hospital at Alcala de Henares. Just a note saying gone to the Front, please bring the refrigerator. Hefting it into the truck and on our way. Passing truck after truck loaded with soldiers. Singing and shouting – bayonets fixed. The red five-pointed star in paint on the side.

"The well-intentioned attempt, by the governments of Britain and France, to limit the fighting in Spain by signing other nations to a non-intervention agreement, seems to have had the opposite effect."

"Necessity is blind until it becomes conscious. Freedom is the consciousness of necessity."

You can ski on almost anything, whether it's slush or crust or ice. Powder is best because it makes you think you're floating. Of course it cushions you if you ever take a fall.

Herding them into the bullring. All of them. Every one. Women, children, grandfathers. A sprinkling of priests. Lining them up against the wall of the barrera. The stench of urine from the horses and the bulls. Planks with faded paint and the scars from the horns. Arms around the little ones. Pulling them into their shoulders. Hands over the eyes and over the ears. Some of the people sit or squat but most of them stand. Not a sound. Not a bird. No droning of warplanes overhead. No one talks except the soldiers who are waiting to start. The lieutenant barks an order. The soldiers jab with their rifles at the people on the flanks. "Move them closer together. In a bunch. We want no strays." A problem with the machine gun? Wrong bullets? A jam in the breach? Why is it taking so long? "It is nothing. Nothing at all. We are ready to start." The slow rising of the arm, the pause and the quick descent. People crying out in terror, people falling, people pleading. The bark, bark, bark of the machine gun as it sweeps from left to right. Some still standing and so it sweeps to the left again. Finally, a pile of arms and legs and bleeding torsos. The lieutenant stabs with his sword when he hears a groan.

Asturian miners in need of anti-tetanus vaccine.
German warships shelling Almeria.
People sheltering in doorways at the sound of planes.

"Bethune has a number of vulnerable chinks in his armour. He was wounded when the nuns of the Sacré Cour told him that God was on Franco's side."

"Dr. Bethune sometimes loses his self-control. When he gets drinking late at night, he often mutters about how things went wrong with his wife."

Action follows thought - the basis of a civilized society - inter-cranial pressure - boys from the trenches on leave - a strange and dangerous road - drive you insane - staggering across the plain - a society without a soul - paintings, fine wines and a roaster - a ditch between the two.

I just had to get out of Canada. I had to seek a wider world. I was so stifled there that at times I couldn't breathe.

I had seen others but I had never seen myself. I had seen Canada but had never seen the world. I thanked Marion for letting me see through her eyes.

Graham Spry was surprised and a little chagrined. He had asked for volunteers for Spain and no one replied. "Well now you have a delegation of one."

A man and dog out walking in the woods.
Of course I am the leader thinks the man.
I am the one who has the better brain.

Passing a string of tanks. Looking slow when seen in the distance but hiking right along as we move out and past. Thirty or forty miles an hour. Waving and honking our horn as we leave the tanks behind. A string of support moving up to the Front. Gasoline trucks, bread wagons, donkey carts, mule trains moving up. A troupe of helmeted Germans. That's the Thaelmann Battalion. They've been using them as shock troops. Must be something big going on or they wouldn't be here.

"While Britain and France have upheld their part of the bargain by preventing the shipment of arms to the Republican side, there is now mounting evidence that Nazi Germany and Fascist Italy are violating the terms of the agreement, which they willingly signed, by sending arms, equipment and combatants to fight for the Fascist cause in Spain."

Sitting down to write a letter to friends about what I have learned.
Wracking my brain, but coming up with nothing at all.

A slope of sparkling snow above a plain.
A document signed with many shades of ink.
A person attempting to paint the depths of his soul.

He crouches down on his hands and knees. Intent on keeping the head down most of all. "The other side has helmets, but we have none. They can use them to scrape the earth. Not even shovels to dig our holes. Just use your hands. Maybe a stick or a broken twig. Just get yourself down as low as you possibly can. The bombardment will keep us pinned down. They'll shred our forces as much as they can. Our job is to keep alive 'til the whistle blows. Then it's up and over the top. Take as many of them as you can. Kick the gun away if you see one beside a corpse. They have a way of playing possum until your back is turned."

Blackened and crumpled bodies lying in rows.
Air bombardments pounding Bilbao.
Anti-Fascist posters pinned to a wall.

He is a man who gives up his own life in service to others.
The comforts of life mean nothing to him at all.

An opening in the frost - delivering the goods - in a neutral café - patch on the inside - the purest motives - living on black bread - turned their backs on us - the forces which seek to overthrow - language can be a problem - the peak of a mountain.

The shooting of every Spaniard who voted for democracy. Slaughtering peasants in the bullrings of the towns. A million orphans out of five million children in Spain.

Blood-transfusion in the trenches. That was the need I saw. How to bring medical help to the wounded before they could die?

Labelling bottles far into the night. Dodging potholes on the Spanish roads. Making a faulty refrigerator perk again.

You have done marvellous well, people told the physician.
You must be proud to have saved a human life.
Your skills must have the blessings of the gods.

Cold wind as we cross the plain. Blowing down from the Guadarramas. Turning up our collars. Every time I look at snow I yearn to ski. That crack in the corner of the windshield. Didn't seem so important in Madrid. A swinging pole from an errant mule-train. The wind whistles as it comes in straight on our faces. This road has an excellent surface. Must be making sixty at least. In half an hour we should see old Franco himself. Sharp left at the top of a hill. There she is. They're supposed to have five hundred beds. Last week the Fascists used the Red Cross for a target.

I am falling from a high mountain. Head over head over heels. I fall into an abyss. Pursued by swarms of bats. Looking up at the magnificent castle. It is a flimsy Hollywood set. I fall and fall and fall. A dark red river flows at the bottom of a canyon.

Quarrels over money, art and friends. Quarrels over medicine, roadsters, gifts. What was it that we never quarrelled about?

Does your soul reside in that painting?
The one you painted late at night when the children were gone?
Were you looking into your soul when you painted your eyes?

Long rows of blood-drenched stretchers. Leaning up against the walls. Waiting to be washed and used again. We jam on the brakes and hit the ground running. Straight up the stairs to the operating room. The thick fumes of ether. Salud to the surgeon and straight to the refrigerator. Empty blood bottles left on top. Seven empties and three unused inside. Just got here in time. We'll leave you six for now. Bring more tomorrow. The surgeon looks up a moment without losing a beat. Where are the tags? The nurse pulls a handful of bottle-tags from her apron. Stuck together and stained with blood. Name, battalion, wound, date of receipt. Out the door and down the hall.

"It is now becoming clear to international observers that Generalissimo Franco, leader of the Fascist forces which are seeking to overthrow the democratically-elected government of the Spanish Republic, is relying on German bombers and Italian tanks to add muscle to the advance of his armies as he attempts to wrest control of the Spanish mainland away from its legitimate rulers."

"We should support whatever the enemy opposes and oppose whatever the enemy supports."

A skier falling into a bank of snow.
A knight tearing a kerchief in two.
A doctor drilling a hole in a cranium.

He is parked on a small bridge. He places the blood ampules in the little mountain stream which trickles under the bridge and forms a pool and then flows away. "Ten minutes of this should be just about right." The driver lights up a smoke and puts his back against a sapling and watches the water as it meets the ampules and flows around them and continues on its way. The perfect place to stop and rest if you were on vacation. The partisans are encamped in the next valley. They are preparing for the next big Franco push. Imagine yourself as a soldier, lying under the stars tonight and dreaming of this cold, clear mountain stream.

Radio speeches written for the raising of funds back home.
A barrage of guns at the Ebro River.
A wounded soldier giving a clenched-fist salute.

"Dr. Bethune is smoking heavily and is obviously under a very considerable strain."

"Bethune is very unhappy in Spain. He is bitter and unhappy working here."

To offer a sacrifice - the price of jewels - do unto others - to reconstruct experience - they set him on fire - eager to break the routines - broken the cardinal rule - the only one on the train - too high for him to climb - an analysis of history.

I kept to my standards. I insisted on telling them what could be improved. Those Spanish doctors were just too Spanish for me.

The Committee in Aid of Spanish Democracy. I assumed that I had their support. I had the illusion that there was rock beneath my feet.

The Communists were the only ones whose motives were pure. Every other belief was for sale. Only the Communists managed to earn my trust.

A light shone on the peak of a mountain.
A peasant climbed to the top.
When he got there, he found a star.
He rolled it down the mountain and it smashed into fragments.

Wounded, doctors, nurses, stretcher-bearers. Doctor Jolley's department. Just in time. The room is packed with the wounded. Bandages on heads and arms and legs. We've got your refrigerator in the car! Great! Bring it inside! Hefting the refrigerator out of the car. Carrying it inside and plugging it in. It shudders and then starts to hum. Four bottles of blood inside. Dr. Jolley's assistant, André. Can you leave me another two needles? Can you spare another syringe? Oh, and how about grouping serums? We'll take whatever you've got.

"There is speculation that Hitler and Mussolini are bargaining with Franco for concessions which will advance their own plans for the march of Fascism beyond their own national borders."

Frances and I, looking at each other through a sheet of ice.
Marion and I, looking at each other through a sheet of glass.

Droning bombers and clanking tanks attacking a town.
A man who is surprised when offered help.

Pasting labels on bottles far into the night.

Rolling over and over in delirium. Trying to write a letter to send back home. *A great, ever-blooming tree. Timeless, indestructible and immortal.* Searching for the ability to explain his deepest thoughts. For the ability to explain what has happened. *He becomes all men in himself. He gives birth to the children of his being.* Struggling to write what he has learned from the ordeal. *He reminds the world of its dark ancestry.* Rolling over and then back. Left to right and left again. The ink will not flow onto the paper. The ground is shifting beneath his feet. Not an iota of a thought as to where to go from here.

The dropping of several tons of bombs.
Clouds of dust and explosive fumes.
Fascist soldiers six miles from Madrid.

He is a man who keeps his eyes below the horizon.
A man for whom human blood is his bread and his wine.

Ancient knowledge - a country giving birth - a voice from across the world - through the nightmare - a bit of a loose cannon - looking carefully at his face - claim the deepest level - prisoners for the rest of the war - the birthplace of all my ideals - a million homeless kids.

May brought money and greetings from Canada. He wrote reams of praise for the work I was doing in Spain. How could I know that his knife was aimed at my back?

I presented my orphanage idea to the Committee for Aid to Spanish Democracy. "Cancel the blood-transfusion unit; it's reached a dead-end. Pour all of the money into an ideal future for Spain."

My experiences are inside me. They have changed me and I want to say how. How to transpose the reality of experience into the reality of the written word?

In the beginning, I made a world, said God.
I made it with the calipers in my hand.
I made darkness on the face of the deep.
Everything I made, I made of chaos;
There is chaos in everything I made.

By the way can you help us out? There's a wounded soldier upstairs. Not English, French, Italian, Spanish or German. Hit by a bomb. Lost a hand. Had to amputate the other. Blinded in one of his eyes. Needs another transfusion. Be nice if someone could speak to him in his own tongue. We all troop into the ward. Big fellow. Six feet tall. Two hundred pounds. A bloody bandage on his head. Two bloody stumps on his arms where there used to be hands. Sorensen steps forward and whispers slowly. The patient's lips are swollen and he struggles to speak. Why he's a Swede! He's speaking Swedish! Tell him he's lost a lot of blood, but he'll be okay. Must have lost a couple of quarts. White face. Feeble pulse. Heat the blood to body temperature. Group his blood. Sterilize the syringe. Blood number 695. Donor 1106. Group IV. Madrid, March 6. All okay. No haemolysis. Here we go. Needle in. Syringe working smoothly. Soon be done. Sorensen soothes him in Swedish. Clean the syringe and pack the bag. Check the pulse. One hundred and strong. Colour better. He'll soon be all right.

The dyer plunges his hand into a vat.

A long line of support moving up to the Front.
A man being chased by a swarm of bats.
A man turning his back on a star.

He swirls the cloth to the right and then to the left.

Avicenna writing his Canon of Medical Knowledge. Descriptions, causes, techniques. Diphtheria, diabetes, cancer and gout.

His hand and wrist are darker than the rest of his arm.

Are you still looking for your soul?
Can it only be seen in reflection?
Will you see it, someday, in the eyes of someone else?

Piling back into the mobile-unit. A pause for breath and then a crank of the engine. She hesitates and then leaps into life. Pulling out and down the road. Back to Madrid to pick up supplies and another run back to the Front with more preserved blood. The cold wind pours in through the crack in the broken windshield. I can see our breath as we talk. By the way, Sorensen, that soldier who lost his two hands. What did he say? I am no more use to my comrades! I have done nothing for the cause! This was my first engagement! Ten days ago I was in Sweden on my father's farm!

Chapter 10

Spain 5

Five short months in Spain. The mobile blood-transfusion service is working smoothly. Five mobile-units, a staff of twenty-five. Doctors, technicians, nurses and chauffeurs. Supplying blood to every sector. Like the milk deliveries back home; only instead of milk, it's blood. Sealed ampules of refrigerated blood; collecting centre; distribution points; front-line service. Proud of the Canadian medical unit. The saving of hundreds of lives – no, make that thousands. The saved returning to the Front to fight for the cause. Bethune in Spain, money from Canada, the mobile-units – all my ducks in a line. The ecstasy of being needed. The thrill of delivering the goods. Taking blood to the wounded! A beautiful – Canadian – idea! The only problem is the Spanish. All the money comes from Canada. Are we only welcome in Spain because we can pay?

A strange and dangerous road lies ahead of me.

A group of people being questioned in a crowded room.
Two people exploring ideas in a coffee shop.
A person climbing upward through an avalanche.

Fear of disharmony is now my greatest fear.

The Haida elder secures the Devil's Club. Diphtheria, pneumonia, cancer and wasting disease. Medicinal, cultural, spiritual healing ensues.

There are things that I must steel myself against.

Has the mobile blood-transfusion concept been patented?
Is it named after Norman Bethune?
Ever think of taking your ball and leaving the field?

Exhausted to the bottom of my shoes. Overwhelmed by the amount of work. Living on black bread and thick coffee. Living on beans and lentils and a piece of fish or two. Money tied up at a bank in Paris. Unable to pay the Spanish doctors. Unable to convey my sense of urgency to the people back home. Unable to break through petty allegiances to a sense of brotherhood. Lack of sleep, lack of money, lack of goodwill. Lying awake in the middle of the night and rubbing my temples. Smoking, taking a drink. What to do?

"Many international observers are amazed that the Franco forces, despite a massive onslaught of troops and firepower, have been unable to overwhelm the staunch defenders of the city of Madrid."

"History does nothing; it does not possess immense riches, it does not fight battles. It is men, real, living, who do all this."

Some days are not good to ski. Some days you can't go on the slopes, though you think you can. Some days you're the only one on the train with a pair of skis.

Toronto traffic outside the window. Clang of the streetcar; squeal of the wheels. The office of the Committee for Aid to Spanish Democracy. "Glad to see you've opted for Spain. We can always use volunteers. There's a lotta work to be done in a worthy cause. See you done some office work. Must mean you know how to read and write. There's a fella we sent to Spain called Doctor Bethune. Claims he's too busy to write for the cause. Working his fingers, he says, to the bone. Says he does medical work at all the major venues. You could attach yourself to him. We'll tell him you'll write him up good. Oh, an let's keep this between ourselves. He's a bit of a loose cannon. Has a lot of peculiar ideas. Just keep your eye on this man, Bethune. Don't let him know you're reporting back to us. That's all you have to do. Important to know the money's being well-spent. Just let us know what you think of this fellow, Bethune."

A seaplane bombing children in a ploughed field.

Coal, meat, milk impossible to obtain.
Homeless orphans begging on the streets.

"Bethune is always complaining of the Spanish doctors. He rails against their lack of commitment and dedication."

"Bethune has broken the cardinal rule. Criticize a surgeon and you've made an enemy for life."

Long, white flowing robes - painting a self-portrait - a survey of their needs - sirens sing their songs - a stage in his life - your thumb on the scale - the fragments of an idea - the honeymoon trip to paris - a world with one-part chaos - a song at the edge of a cliff.

But now that I think it over, I'd have to say that I got it wrong. Sure Canada disappointed me, but it started me on my path. Canada was the birthplace of all my ideals.

Marion was married but I didn't need a wife. Marion was looking inward and I was looking outside. When we hugged, we both knew it was right to say goodbye.

The formation of the Committee to Aid Spanish Democracy. Appeals for help to all interested parties. The next thing I knew I was on a boat for Spain.

Young Proffit snarled at the worker whom he had just fired.
I caught you talking to another worker!
This means that neither of you has been properly doing his job!

The Spanish doctors and their jealousy. They think I stole the idea of the blood transfusion from them. But they based themselves in a hospital in Barcelona. Soldiers were dying on their way there from the Front. It never occurred to them to put the whole operation on wheels. And I haven't been self-promoting. Sure I write about what I've been doing. I send it out to the world. The films and photographs are my means of raising funds. The jealousy and incompetence of the Spanish doctors. I tell them what I think. It's the only way they'll improve. The disappointment of working with people who are not like me.

"The Franco forces are now engaged in a pincer movement in an attempt to dominate central Spain, and to force the Republican government to retreat from Madrid to Barcelona."

Sitting at my typewriter with only the fragments of an idea.
Trying to make a simple sentence out of all this debris.

An explorer on a cold and lonely mission.

A god creating a world with one-part chaos.
A man and woman exchanging a hug and saying goodbye.

The doctor is being questioned. The members of the mobile-unit; an interrogation room. Some allegations for the doctor to confirm or deny. *"*Is she your nurse or your secretary?" "Did she tell you she was an Austrian? No Austrian, we have been told, speaks English like that!" *Wearing trousers and riding a motor-bike. A dashing figure in the war.* "Why would she ask suspicious questions about a bridge?" *A striking appearance and a warm nature. A golden giantess with windblown hair.* "Why would you take her on your travels delivering blood?" *A blanket spread out on the rocks, a gurgling mountain stream, taking turns sipping whiskey from a shared glass.* "How do you know she's not an anarchist or a spy?"

Parents shielding their children by lying on top of them.
A bomber pilot dying of his wounds.
Eight thousand civilians killed by bombardments.

He is a giant who strides among pygmies.
A man of vision whose fellows have often let him down.

Tearing a kerchief in two - eenee, meenie, minie, moe - the favour in her eyes - to entertain a risk - writing in white-hot heat - a scratching sound - the war inside myself - a deserted town - obedient, proud and strong - shade and sunlight dance.

What is a doctor if not a healer? What are we born for if not to save lives? How could a doctor read the news and not go to Spain?

I put two and two together. Advances in the methods of storing blood and the need for blood at the Front. That is the idea I had when I was in Spain.

Blood-out on the battlefield. Blood-in through a needle in the arm. Blood was death and blood was life in those days in Spain.

Death sat alone with his drink in a tavern.
Outside the window, his pale horse munched his oats.
I have tried to cut down Pestilence but to no avail.
I need a less-formidable foe to destroy.

The politics of saving lives. The constant political manoeuvring. The constant fighting for control. The disdain for serving under a foreigner. The jealousy, the superstition, the secret reports sent to superiors. Not a faithful Communist! Disregard for the good of the cause! Bethune and his nurse act like spies! They make notes as they travel the roads! They note the locations of troops!

They make diagrams of the terrain! They say it is for medical purposes, but how can we know?

The knight looked at the maiden, the young girl says to her young man. A cloud formed over his countenance. He drew and kissed his gleaming sword, and then he descended the stone steps – down, down, down – into the lion's den. He killed the lion, returned to the maiden, tore the scented kerchief in two and thrust half of it at her feet. Then he mounted his faithful steed and turned his back on the favour in her eyes.

You can't go back; you must go forward. Whatever has been cannot be undone. That is the blessing and the curse from the earliest times.

Were you born to be a statue made of bronze?
Looking far out over the heads of everyone?
Far above the grit and the grind of the everyday?

The loss of the blood-transfusion unit. A message to Doctor Bethune. The Spanish government is bringing the Canadian unit under its control. There will be no more independent units. You will report to Spanish doctors, to the Sanidad Militar. How can they take my unit away? Why the need to seize control? What next? Erase "Canadiense" from the sides of the mobile-units? Are we not international brothers? Is the war only being fought for Spain? Keep the Canadian money flowing! Money from Canada will still be welcome, but not Bethune! Writing back home to Canada. Writing in white-hot heat. Advising that our work here is at an end! Advising that the money be discontinued! Advising withdrawal of the Bethune blood-transfusion unit completely from Spain!

"German Hinkel bombers and Italian tri-motor bombers continue to rain death on the cities of Spain. Despite the fact that many of their nationals have flocked to the Republican banner, the signing of the non-intervention treaty means that the governments of the democratic nations have remained neutral in the battle for the soul of Spain."

"Every war exacts a price, sometimes an extremely high one."

A man on a powdery slope with a pair of skis.
A man falling head over heels into an abyss.
A typewriter with a blank page in an empty room.

The doctor leans against the wall and lights a cigarette. He takes a drag – deep, deep – and sucks it, satisfyingly, into his lungs. Broken bricks and piles of plaster litter the courtyard. The Canadian doctor is a mad-man. Always ranting;

always raving. Throwing his gloves down on the floor and stomping away. Why have those bottles not been cleaned? Why is that crate still unopened over there? Is there anyone here who has learned a single thing? Muttering plans to build an orphanage. Far up in the hills of Spain. Green grass! Blue skies! Gentle rain! He shouted in my face the other day. Well, I am a doctor too. I have my integrity. I no longer wish to work with Doctor Bethune.

Buildings engulfed in a reddish-orange glow.
A woman sitting in a pool of blood and suckling a child.
People paying their telephone bills while the building is being shelled.

"Bethune is drinking an awful lot. He suffers from insomnia and says he has nightmares."

"Bethune is a man who is over-stressed. He can't get the Spanish to do what he wants them to do."

Great black pears - have remained neutral - a war-time truce - the grit and the grind - saving the bruised and the torn - what do you fear most - two people exploring ideas - according to the rules - eden still unploughed - a surging of the pulse.

Word sent to my supporters back home in Canada. "The Spanish doctors don't like to work with Bethune." That was the end of my service to the people of Spain.

I was too busy giving blood-transfusions to watch my back. I didn't know that I wore a target. When the fatal blow was delivered, it came as a shock.

Capitalism had failed. It had abandoned the common man. Communism was the only belief that made sense to me.

I have decided what I will do, said the second man.
I will walk along the road towards the victim.
I will avert my eyes and pass by on the other side.

Confrontation in Madrid. Stabbed in the back by Sorensen, Sise, May. Your drinking! Your anger! Your relationship with the nurse! Your rage! Your poor diet! Your lack of sleep! Your conflict with the Spanish doctors! Your independence! Your lack of respect! Your complaints about inefficiency and indolence! You are poisoning the enterprise! We wrote a letter to our sponsors in Canada. Recommending that you be recalled from Spain. We would be better off without you. We believe that your time for doing good here has passed.

"While the defense of Madrid is certainly gallant, the rifles and machine guns of its Republican defenders are seen by objective observers as a fragile bulwark against the potential for devastation of the German and Italian bombers. Others hold out the hope, despite the recent Republican losses, that a world war can be averted if Fascism can be defeated in Spain."

What to write to my friends back home?
All I can picture is a field of broken debris.

A man lying awake in the middle of the night.
A black horse munching oats outside a tavern.
A man lying on a stretcher and bleeding to death.

He rolls over in his sleep. Fragments of thoughts inside his head. *The negation of the negation. Not a flat, circular movement. A turn and return on itself.* As dead end – as blind – as any brick wall he has ever come up against. *The union of life and death. The medium is vivified.* Desperate for an idea. *The emergence of the new from the old; the retaining of the old within the new.* His pillow is drenched in sweat. The open window brings no relief. A man without an idea at the end of the world.

Parked beside a cool mountain stream.
Heaps of huddled clothes on cobblestones.
Poetry written against the horrors of the war.

He is a man for whom new worlds are always waiting.
He is a man for whom the darkness is never profound.

At work in the world today - in the glow of the star - the fight will go on - into an abyss - the lashing of wind and rain - two friendly equals - heavy fighting today - a man who is over-stressed - to fend for themselves - a person climbing upward.

Sorensen, Sise and May. All three of them held the knife. They plunged it right between my shoulder-blades.

They said "no" to my idea. "We'll fund the blood-transfusion unit, but not an orphanage." They refused to rescue the broken children of Spain.

I have my pen and my paper. The typewriter sits on the desk. I think for hours but I do not write a single word.

A voice spoke to the doctor in a dream.
Physician, heal thyself! the voice ordered.
Oh, I can do that, the doctor replied.
I will eliminate the Hippocratic Oath.

A telegram from Canada. To Doctor Norman Bethune – Barcelona, Spain. From the Committee to Aid Spanish Democracy. The people who sent me here. A rag-tag combination of liberals, socialists and communists. Fighting like dogs at home but joining to send me to Spain. United – temporarily – for a common cause. An alliance of animosities. Their support is a shifting rug. Cold ink on a piece of paper. All of their principles swept aside. Canadian liberals, socialists and communists agree on one thing. If the Spanish don't like Bethune – let's bring him home.

She places a wet cloth on the child's forehead.

Blood being delivered as if it is milk.
Peasants firing rifles at a distant plane.
A man cramming his belongings into a duffle-bag.

She snuggles her face into its neck and coos a tune.

Esagil-kin-apli of Babylon. Diagnosis, prognosis, physical examination and medical prescription. Writing his concepts down as a medical text.

The eyes of the child are blurred and it has no smile.

Can you see yourself as Sorensen, Sise or May?
Can you see yourself as looking through their eyes?
How could you ask them to cease the blood-transfusions in Spain?

There's nothing for you here in Spain. What about fundraising for us in Canada? You'll be much more valuable there. Montreal, Toronto, Windsor. A swing through the West and the USA. Publicity for the cause wherever you go. Speeches, interviews, rallies. Stories of the blood-transfusion unit and how many lives have been saved. The last bastion against the Fascists and the raised-fist salute. But for God's sake don't say you're a Communist! They won't give a dime if they know what you are! No doubt you'd rather stay here, but here you have done about all that you can. Your reputation will still be secure. It will still say "Canadiense" on the mobile units, as the photos will show. You can't blame the Spanish doctors. It's only natural for the Spanish to want control. For all the good you've done, to them you're still a foreigner on Spanish soil. Look, I think the same way as you, but all this comes down from somewhere above. Surely you'll sacrifice for the cause. Surely you'll do what's best for us all. You'll be much more valuable in Canada than you are here in Spain. It would be best for you to leave Spain just as soon as you can.

Chapter 11

China 1

Awakening at 3:00 a.m. We have stopped. Darkness. Where can we be? Chatter in Chinese outside. Rolling over on a bag of rice and peering through the slats of the boxcar. A group of soldiers and the engineer in the light of a torch. Sliding down the bags of rice and crawling over to the door. Raising the latch and sliding it open enough to squeeze through. My interpreter sliding with me. Jean Ewen remaining inside. We'll let you know. The officer glancing aside at me without missing an angry word. He says we have four hundred bags of rice. Must not be let to fall into the hands of Japanese. Must get to the Eighth Route Army before they attack. Engineer says he will go no farther. Yesterday the train was buzzed a number of times by Japanese planes. Probably hoping their troops will catch us and take the rice. Hot day coming today. We will have to walk. We will cross the river into Shensi and then walk to Yan'an. The engine chuffs and puffs as it waits by the siding on the track. Engineer says the train will not go on.

To paint or to write is a form of action.

A dyer mixing up a vat of dye.
An explorer on a cold and lonely mission.

A great field overrun with choking weeds.

To work in blood and bone is action too.

The writing of texts in the heart of ancient China. Shen Nong's Canon of Herbs. The Yellow Emperor's Canon of Interior Medicine. Herbs, acupuncture and massage.

One form of action at a time is enough – I cannot do both.

Moving a hill with just a shovel?
Moving a mountain with just a spoon?
Do you ever wonder why others don't bother to try?

Walking along beside a long line of mules. Clear, dry air. A brilliant day. It took all day to unload the rice from the train and put it in carts. The Japanese are getting close. About one hundred of our soldiers came shuffling towards us from along the railway line. Jean and I bandaged up the wounded while my interpreter gave me the news. Explosions thundered down the line as the rice was unloaded. The Japanese are advancing. Our troops are holding them off as best they can. Village after village is deserted. Only a few have decided to stay. Can anything be worse than what we have now? Four hundred bags of rice. Forty-two carts. Three mules apiece, two mules in the lead and one between the shafts. Two hundred miles to the Yellow River. Village gates are closed and barred. We are forced to go around. No food or water for our soldiers and our drivers. Silent pairs of eyes stare over the walls.

"The Japanese invasion of northern China appears to be quite successful. The superiority of the Japanese military juggernaut seems to meet very little resistance from the Chinese. The Japanese Imperial Army is now in possession of Peiping and most of the province of Hopei and is now driving west and south into rural China."

"Give away all that you have and follow me."

I have never skied in China. I have never skied here at all. Yet all the best conditions are all around me. The loftiest of mountains and the loveliest snow.

A line of plodding mules, each one saddled with bags of precious rice. Setting out for Sian. A distance of two hundred and twenty-five miles. I feel completely fresh. The ride on the train was a picnic. Someone told me that the Great Trek – from the South to the North – was eight thousand miles. I learned to sing The Marseillaise. The northern hills were strange to me, a rickshaw man from the streets of Shanghai. A pleasant day for marching. My legs are now like trees. The wheat is up and the sun brings along a cool breeze.

Primitive, understaffed, under-supplied.
A long march of eight thousand miles.
Millet, turnip, cabbage, mutton, pork.

"Dr. Bethune has given up on Canada. He is a man who is always shedding his own skin."

"Dr. Bethune was very lonely and unhappy in Canada. By going to China, he is running away from himself."

A fragile bulwark - not a mode of living - the way they think - to crack an egg - I saw it all differently - an unseen element - to remain independent - a field of broken debris - struggling along a road - the saving of hundreds of lives.

Touring Canada and the United States. Giving speeches and raising money for the fight against Fascism. Stressing the unity of the Republican cause in the fight to save Spain.

What in the world to say about Spain? Mission aborted; credit denied. Almost everything I did was thrown back in my face.

Plenty of work for a doctor in China. Plenty of agony and disease. If you want to get your hands dirty, it's the place to be.

Scour the earth from stem to stern, the great god told the messenger.
All I can see is misery, carnage and pain.
Look for one good person who is doing one good deed.

Walking along beside the lead cart. A droning overhead. Two Japanese bombers going south, about a half a mile away. A thousand feet in the air. Not interested? Don't see us? No such luck. The second bomber wags his wings. He comes down to five hundred feet and inspects our line. Forty-two carts, a line of mules, a line of wounded soldiers. No anti-aircraft guns. No Chinese planes. We all scramble for cover and dig in as best we may. One bomber stays high and one flies down to look. We are lying on the ground – flat and unprotected. Not a tree, not a stone, not a gully, nor a hill, nor a rock-formation to hide behind. Five old rifles and fifty men. Drivers, boys and wounded and Jean and I. The bomber passes down the line and then flies back to the head of our line. He comes down to two hundred feet and drops four bombs. He seems to miss by fifty feet, but the mules flinch and some of them drop to their knees. He comes back again and drops four bombs near the end of our line. Then the bombers fly away.

A man looking at a mountain with a spoon in his hand.

Four men wounded, fifteen mules killed and twelve wounded. The bombs break up as they hit and spray everything two feet above the ground for a hundred feet. Many wounds on the legs of the mules. We had no time to dig a trench. Jean and I dress the wounded. The shrapnel has taken a toll. A soldier with a piece of a bomb in his back. A driver with a piece of steel passing though his arm and out at the armpit. The Japanese army must be close. They will report our location and have their troops come for the rice. Four hours of putting things right. Cutting out the dead mules. Shifting the bags of rice. Twenty carts now instead of twenty-four. A wounded driver weeps at the loss of his mules.

"The Japanese armies appear to have consolidated their control over most of the railways of the northern provinces of Hopei, Chahar and Shansi. These railway lines control the lives of thirteen million people over a land mass of one hundred thousand square miles."

Raising funds in Canada for Spain.
Declaring myself to be a Communist and proud to be so.

An army closing in on a shipment of rice.
A doctor selling bandages for a dollar each.
A man moving towards a distant beacon.

They are lying on scraps of straw on a cold, stone floor. Crawling with lice; bloodied uniforms; covered in dirt. Washed-out bandages of faded rags. One blanket to cover three. Boiled millet once a day while they wait to die. The family is kind, but they are almost starving themselves. A lantern in the darkness. One of them stirs and opens his eyes. A man is stooping and bathing my wounds. The warm water on my legs is almost heavenly. "A doctor from Canada", someone says. There are so many of us to care for. Hundreds of wounded lie sick in this village. Only miles from the Japanese. What good can a doctor from Canada possibly do?

Daily lectures to doctors and nurses.
A deluge of sick and wounded soldiers.
Fly control, sterilization, incineration.

He is a man who is up to his elbows in the issues of life.
He is a man for whom a peasant has the value of a king.

A perfect day on the slopes - a man without an idea - my sense of urgen-
cy - a very compassionate soul - a neanderthal grandfather - medicinal herbs
in a garden - two people melting together - pass by on the other side - the blood

brothers - an all-embracing eye.

There were people dying in Spain. They were bleeding to death on the battlefield. I had seen it in the war in 1915.

There were people dying in China. They were dying on the battlefield. They died before they could be operated on.

There are those who say that to be human is to suffer. There are those who say that to be human is to live a life of pain. There are those who insist that this is the way life is.

The leader continued his oration to the troops.
We shall bomb their women and children.
We must do this for the cause.
It is essential to achieve our victory.

Dust. Exhaustion. Bitter cold at night and blazing heat by day. Deserted villages, empty fields. Walking all the way to the Yellow River. The enemy twenty-five miles behind, in close pursuit. Not a single medical officer. Not an ambulance. Two wounded carried on a stretcher. A man with a wound in his thigh on a bullock cart. Buying gauze and cotton and crystals of potassium permanganate in the towns we come to. Using up our morphine tablets. Hundreds of wounded in the last few days. Not a single case of a serious leg wound. Only one head injury – a bullet through the jaw. All the wounds are to hands and arms. All of the other wounded have died or been killed or captured. Medical help is almost nil. I am treating only those who can make their way from the battle field on their own two legs. Few blankets or bedding rolls. Undressed, suppurating wounds. Lack of food. We give them our coins to buy some rice. In a race with the Japanese. They are moving faster than we. Better equipped, better fed, better medical service, presumably. Which one will reach the Yellow River first? I could be captured before my work in China begins.

Lying in the depths. Looking upward. A castle on a high mountain. A Red Cross flag. A bronze statue. Warriors guarding the gate. Climbing slowly up to the castle. Gaining entrance. A little cottage under the trees. The notes of an old happy song.

Frances and I in the mountains of Switzerland. Both of us learning to ski. Both of us laughing as we fall all over the place.

Why concern yourself with these issues?
Are there not other things to do?
Do you think you can cure the ills of all humankind?

Walking along beside the carts. A young lad walking along ahead of me. Every once in a while he stops to rest. Coming abreast of him and taking note. My interpreter talks to him and talks to me. He has been walking in this condition for a week. No help where he was wounded. In agony with every breath he takes. A child of seventeen. An old dark bloodstain on his faded blue jacket. Shot through the lung a week ago. The bullet came out the back. No dressing on the wound. I stop him and take him aside and examine him. Right anterior chest wall. Suppurating badly. Fluid in the pleural cavity. Up to the third rib in front. The heart is displaced three inches to the left. Let's get him on a cart. He can ride on a bag of rice. I'll give him what I can to ease the pain. He moans as the mule-cart jostles on the bumpy road. Coughing painfully as we make our way along. I walk along beside him. Clouds of dust and the draining heat of the sun.

"There seems to be no stopping the juggernaut of the Japanese Imperial Army in its drive to conquer China. Most of the provincial Chinese armies have either been defeated in battle or are in full retreat. Municipal and provincial Chinese governments have ceased to operate and their officials have abandoned their posts. Reports are that the Chinese losses in these clashes have been great."

"Learn from the masses, and then teach them."

Frightened peasants peering over walls.
An enclave of lions roaring for prey.
A young boy walking for miles with an open wound.

What is this, in the corner of the field, sticking out of the ground? He walks over to see what it is. It looks like a big black turnip with its top cut off. No! It's a shell! From the big guns of the Japanese. I have seen them up close, once before, at the railway station. I was forced to unload a whole railcar-load for the Japanese. My son spoke of such a gun when he was last home. It had been captured in a skirmish. He falls on his knees and begin to scoop the earth away. I can haul it with my donkey! I can put it in one of the wicker-baskets and balance on the other side with a basket of earth! I will take this to my son! He is with the partisans! Their own shell will be used to fight the Japanese!

Pulmonary tuberculosis, ovarian cyst, gastric ulcer.
A lack of medical officers and materials.
A people devoid of vanity or ambition.

"Bethune is a man who lives a life of drama. He is an actor who is rehearsing his greatest role."
"Dr. Bethune is an internationalist. He recognizes no race, no colour, no language – no boundaries that separate and divide."

*Women, children and old people - talking to yourself - the voices of peo-
ple in pain - no streetlights and no moon - the eyes of the child - crave the respect
- seeds of the human flaw - the only person - people who are not like me - please
save my child.*

General Nieh is a brilliant General in the 8th Route Army. I saw myself as
a brilliant general in the field of health. It was like locking horns with a version
of myself.

I was honest and open in my reports to Comrade Mao. I told him my
every thought. I told him exactly what I wanted to do and how I proposed to do
it.

I spent very little time with Comrade Mao. I only met him once, for a
very brief time. Comrade Mao is a very busy man.

*The people met in the courtyard during the day.
The wolf is getting bigger each time we feed him, someone said.
There is not one animal left for our offering tonight.*

Crowding in on the banks of the Yellow River. Pursued by the Japanese.
At last I have caught up to the Eighth Army. My goal since I left Canada, a
month ago. Dressing the wounded who congregate here. Only those who have
made their way back. Nothing but neglected minor injuries. All the seriously
wounded have died on their way from the Front. A walk through the local town.
Carp in water in buckets for sale. Bark-less dogs. Paper windows. Black pigs
with big floppy ears. I go to see the local doctor. Doctor, dentist and druggist all
in one. A quack of the worst kind. A shop full of wounded, waiting for dressings.
Charging each soldier a dollar for every bandage. Charging me four dollars for
a roll of gauze. East bank of the Yellow River. Men and goods on the river bank.
The Japanese are getting closer. They burned the village that we passed through
yesterday. Pitch black. No moon in the sky. Dozens of fires blazing brightly.
Men, mules, carts, trucks, horses, artillery. Piles of goods waiting to be ferried
across. The light of the fires reflecting on the mountainside. The river rushing
between two cliffs. The current is twelve miles an hour. Ice-flows smash against
each other in the dark. Climbing on some rice bags and drifting off to sleep. In
the belt of the soldier beside me – a hand grenade.

"There seems to be little resistance in China to the onslaught of the Japanese armies. The Japanese Imperial Government, in Tokyo, announces victory
after victory in their drive south and west. The Japanese control all of the major
railway and road corridors in the occupied territories. The only resistance from
the Chinese seems to be local and on a very small scale."

Walking in the mountains – no stoves, beds or baths.
Dirt and lice, punishing heat and bitter cold.

A man giving speeches for a doubtful cause.
A man pointing his finger at another man.
A mother howling her words in the pelting rain.

Three o'clock in the morning. December 1, North China, near Lin Chu, with the 8th Route Army. *The innumerable tiny cells of the body.* The kerosene lamp is buzzing. Mud walls, paper windows, mud floor. Men with wounds. *The memory of a million years. Other tides, other oceans, life being born of the sea and the sun.* Why is sleep so hard to come-by? He exhausts himself by day. He cannot refresh himself at night. *Drink deep and struggle back into life again.* The smell of blood and chloroform. Cold despite the fire. Old filthy bandages stuck to the skin with black-blood glue.

Bandages washed until they are nothing but rags.
Stretcher-bearers carrying a wounded man all day.
Communism as the force that moves the heart.

He is a man for whom every drop of blood is precious.
A man who renews our original gift from God.

In the shadow of the parthenon - no patience with incompetence - a sick daughter - blood of brothel and mud - people like black ants - a form of action - skiing downhill on a sunny day - things as they are - the epic struggle - whiskey from a shared glass.

I don't know what happened to Jean Ewen. She sent the shipment of equipment on ahead and didn't come with it. The boys who brought the shipment didn't seem to understand what she had said.

Precision has always been my watchword. It has been the key to everything I have done. Whether operating in the heat of battle or cooking an egg.

The peaceable society will someday come about. Every person will be equal. Ever resource will belong to all.

If you do not choose to measure gold and silver,
Then, my friend, why not throw the scales away?

Awake at five A M. Cold and overcast. Four junks to take us all. It will take four days to get us all to safety! The Japanese are ten miles away! We are ordered into the first junk. Fifty feet long and twenty-five feet wide. A hundred people on board with artillery, mules and baggage. The current sweeps us downstream. We bump against the ice-flows. The air is cold. We find an eddy near the bank. A boy jumps aboard with a pole and slows us down. The current takes us to the bank and we scramble on shore. Troops in trenches, batteries of field guns. Automatic rifles, machine guns, hand grenades. A junk of wounded soldiers soon sweeps in behind. River rising, bitter wind, choppy waters. Many are waiting on the opposite bank for their chance to cross. In the distance, we can hear the Japanese guns.

A man beginning a journey with a single step.

A letter to Comrade Mao. I envision a model hospital. An idea I first had when I was in Spain. Safe behind our lines. Ideal in all its facilities. I, of course, would be in charge. I would train volunteer medical personnel. There would be a ripple effect. Each in turn would train others in the field. It is the best way I can think of to help the cause. It will strengthen the Eight Route Army by returning soldiers to the fight. I will personally cover all costs. All of the money will come from Canada and the United States.

One woman works alone at the edge of the group.

A junk in a strong current being swept downstream.
A bomber dropping bombs on a train of mules.
A young boy who is learning to cook an egg.

She cries as she slaps the cloth on the stones.

A Roman doctor lays out his instruments. Forceps, scalpels, cautery, cross-bladed scissors, surgical needle. On the tripod a pot of water boils.

None of the other women laughs or smiles.

An end to dictatorship, oppression, torture?
Does Jesus not say that the poor will always be with you?
Why lift a finger, then, if what he says is true?

Japanese troops on the bank across from us. Our field guns firing over our heads. The lashing of wind and rain. We struggle to haul our supplies up from the shore. Machine gun bullets pop in the water as we work. Slogging up the slope and dumping over into a trench. Working in a cave in the side of a hill. Forty feet deep in the ground. Dressing wounded men. Outside it starts to snow. A fire crackles and the cave is warm. The constant noise of the explosions. Japanese shelling from the opposite bank. A child with convulsions. Soap stick enema as a cure. The mother rushing out in the rain and howling the child's name.

Working through the night. Wounded soldiers are brought in as the battle rages. Digitalis, adrenalin. Sutures, syringes, cocaine. Once in a while, a break for a mouthful of millet.

Chapter 12

China 2

The model hospital at Sung-yen Kou. Sitting in the courtyard and typing in the morning in the sunshine. A deserted Buddhist temple. Pine trees and a rocky grove. A clear-running mountain stream. Steep mountains north and south, topped with clouds. The Buddhist priests are still here, clinging to the ruins of their temple. At times I hear their chants and gongs and bells. The smell of joss sticks and jasmine in the air. Completed – plans to performance – in only five weeks. The builders sang their revolutionary songs. An operating theatre. A sanitation department. Playing-fields for recuperating patients. Everything at which I smiled as I dreamed. A cookhouse, a games room, a lecture hall, a medical school. A centralized sterilizing plant, a drying oven, a laundry, an incinerator, an operating room, a drug and gauze room, a doctors' office, temperature charts and records. Doctors, nurses, orderlies. Volunteers, civilian nurses, some old and some no more than just a child. Faithfulness and devotion to the cause. Civilians in the village billeting the staff and the wounded. Everyone sees the value of the plan.

All my life my mind has been on fire.

A doctor turning away patients who have no cash.

A man extracting blood from his own arm.
The organizing principle of a single drop of water.

Compassion is the fuel which makes it glow.

Healers toiling in a Mayan medicine garden. The benefits of herbs,
bushes, trees. Chicory, Calendula, Aloe Vera, Amaranth.

A thought has the power to cut through rock.

Are you proud of your model hospital?
Did they reject this concept in Spain?
Have you reported to Comrade Mao on what you have done?

Writing my first textbook. The first of many. The duties of doctors, orderlies, nurses. What are the qualities that a leader must possess? How am I serving in the war? Am I doing it well? Am I doing it as well as it can be done? Can
I do more to help? Outlining the treatment of wounds. Am I doing this dressing
correctly? What is the reason for this way? Is there a better way to do it? The
practice of good technique. Quickly-cured patients? Less pain? Less discomfort?
Less death? Less disease? Less deformity? How can I achieve these ends? So
many things that medical workers need to know.

"After years of partisan bickering, the Chinese, in the face of the over-
whelming strength of the Japanese threat to independence, have decided to form
an alliance of all factions who are determined to help China shake itself free of
the Japanese noose."

"The guerrilla must move amongst the people as a fish swims in the
sea."

Spring skiing is ideal for me. You get those perfect-weather days and the
snow-base is winter-deep and there's not too many people on the slopes.

A boy with frosty breath, sitting close to a fire. He roasts some meat
on a stick and enjoys his uniform. Blue and snug and warm. He has been given
an ancient spear. If someone dies, he will be given a rifle. His leaders explain
the campaign. We sting him at the Front; we sting him in the rear; we attack his
supply lines and vanish like a swarm of wasps. The invaders do not know it, but
the Japanese army is slowly bleeding to death. I am learning to read and to write.
If there is food, my stomach is filled; if there is none, we are all the same. The
commanders eat or starve along with the troops. He smiles as he thinks of the
future. After the war, I will stay in the army. A better life, for me, than back on

the farm.

Respiratory infection, frostbite, trachoma.
Thirty miles from the battle to the hospital.
Hundreds huddled in the rain on a river bank.

"Dr. Bethune is giving inspiration to many thousands of medical workers. They strive to emulate his spirit of service to the sick and the wounded."

"Dr. Bethune is unhappy when he loses a patient. He doesn't cry but he certainly does get mad."

Advances in the methods - one's greatest task - a man lying on a stretcher - a pleasant day for marching - to become a monk - the girl tells a story - an india-rubber ball - a man of great obsessions - the dyer's dog asleep - the pain inside their own skull.

"The world war has already started. Fascism must be defeated in Spain. This can only be done if we present a united front."

There was no getting back with Frances. Frances was herself; I was myself. That was the crime.

Peasants slaughtered by the thousands. Strafing planes and bombing raids. Shooting farmers in the rice paddies and seizing their land.

A man and dog out walking in the woods.
He would be lost without me thinks the dog.
He would be lost without me thinks the man.

The reluctance of the Chinese to give their blood. Needing blood for my transfusions. Getting angry and shouting. What is wrong with you people? Can't you see this is saving lives? Ordering two orderlies to hold a man while I take some blood. He struggles as the men force him to lie down. I shout at him and he stops struggling and I slide the needle in and extract the blood. His face is white as a sheet as he gets up from the table. The rest is a matter of moments. Saving the patient's life, but still concerned. Why are these people staring at me? What is it that makes them reluctant? The Spanish peasants lined up to give their blood! They could see the patient rise as if back from the dead! Fear of contagion? Loss of the self? Loss of the soul? Thinking about the problem. Rolling up my sleeve. A group of peasants standing round in awe. The foreigner is rolling up his sleeve! The doctor is offering his blood! I slide the needle in and extract my own blood. I glance around at the faces as the needle fills. Three hundred cc everybody! A harmless and painless procedure! See, it doesn't hurt at all! The peasants chatter among themselves for a few minutes. Rolling down my sleeve and looking around. A man comes forward, then a woman, then a third. They are sliding their sleeves up their arms. If the foreigner gives his blood, why shouldn't we?

"The various Chinese factions have called for a conference of all peoples' organizations and military forces in the regions of Shansi, Hopei and Chahar provinces, in order to form a united and representative government."

Giving away my clothing to the wounded.
Riding seventeen miles to check on a wounded soldier.

A person catching flies with a slab of honey.
A person on a pair of skis plunging over the edge.
Soldiers walking for days with open wounds.

He stands for a moment and looks over the homestead. The Japanese are coming. What more to hide and what else to leave behind? The mattock, the plough, the harrow. All safely hidden with the mule. Rakes, baskets, earthenware pots. The winter's store of grain. There must be nothing for their army to burn or to steal. The terrace is in stubble; nothing there for an army to eat. Surely the land will still be here when the Japanese leave. The pig and the thirteen hens, the sheep and the goat. All safely hidden in a cave, higher up in the hills. He looks along the valley. No activity on the trail. He pokes his head in the hut and looks around. The little grey pot in which she makes the tea. She still has a few tea-leaves left. He picks it up and tucks it into his coat and turns to the door. Tonight, at least, we will have our cup of tea.

Exhausted, dust-covered, grey-faced men and boys.
No beds, no anaesthetics, no dressings.
Immediate needs, future needs, urgent needs.

If life were fair, he would have no profession.
He would be taken up, like a prophet, into the clouds.

The howls of a young child - find favour in my eyes - encounter the ghost - the politics of saving lives - talking through glass - a modern priestly craft - making up lyrics - shedding his own skin - to build a united front - a jaunty roadster.

I could have stayed in Canada and let the rest of the world suffer. I could have remained where I was and lived the good life. I decided that I could not live with myself as I was.

I knew what the problem was. It was the distance and time between the suffering of the wound and the operation. Many soldiers would walk for days with no attention at all.

There are those who are only concerned for their own community. There are those who are only concerned for their own family. There are those who are only concerned for their own selves.

What have you done? people cried to the physician.
You have saved the worst man in the district.
Countless widows and orphans will suffer because of you.

Getting the model hospital on its feet. One hundred and fifteen operations. Writing two books on surgery and medicine. Writing a weekly medical bulletin for the Front-line medical service. Little time for writing letters. Organizing a publicity bureau. Establishing a department to collect and rewrite articles for the domestic and foreign press. Putting Teng, my interpreter, in charge. Each member is pledged to write at least one article a month. It is important that we tell the world what is happening here. Plans to buy a movie camera when funds permit. We will make films of the army and their heroic resistance. No mail from Canada for months. No letters, no magazines, no newspapers. Why don't they send more help to China? Can't they see that this is the same war we fought in Spain?

Every day, the maiden visits the den where the blood-thirsty lions roar for prey. She holds the torn half-kerchief in her hand and stares down at the lions' fanged maws.

Frances and I on the train to Vienna. Young people all around us, eating sandwiches out of paper bags. Sleeping on each other's shoulders all the way home.

Did you appreciate Jean Ewen?
Did you not make super-human demands?
Did she not choose to serve elsewhere because of you?

Two wounded Japanese prisoners. The light of fear in their eyes. What will happen now? Why have we been brought here? An officer of rank. A badly wounded leg. Sliding him onto the table. Saving his leg and his life. He bows when he recovers, though his eyes are quiet. The other soldier has a cut on the head. The business end of a bayonet. Treated and bandaged and put in place to be healed. Taking photographs with the two. Doctor Lin and two Japanese. Doctor Bethune and two Japanese. A little propaganda of our own. Your gratitude has been noted. Please tell your fellow Japanese. Someday you'll go home and tell everybody what happened here. Chinese and Japanese. No words can pass between them. The only communication is the bow.

"The conference of patriotic Chinese at Fu Ping includes provincial government and Koumintang officials; military leaders of the Central Government and the 8th Route Army; delegates of workers, mass organizations, a Peasants' Union, unions of women and youth, and representatives of the Communist Party."

"Political power grows out of the barrel of a gun."

A group of people forming an alliance.
A man robbing another of money and clothes.
Sirens luring a sailor onto the rocks.

He opens a package that has just come in with a pack-train of mules. An x-ray machine without a dynamo and without the iron upright that is needed to make it work. Wondering what things must be like back home. Is Roosevelt still President of the United States? Who is the Prime Minister of England? Is the Communist Party now in power in France? An opened tin of Canadian cigarettes, a bar of chocolate, a tin of cocoa, a tube of shaving soap. Some parts of letters are missing. Parts of the pages torn away. The curiosity of the censors. What are the secrets that my letters once contained?

Dysentery, syphilis, tuberculosis.
No convalescent homes or rest camps.
Codeine, morphine, copper sulphate.

"Dr. Bethune eats the same food as the soldiers. He insists on the same living conditions as everyone else."
"Dr. Bethune has refused to accept any money for himself. He has directed that all such money be used to buy tobacco for the wounded."

This type of treatment - to abandon all this - a word or two - when I got outside - the scene of the action - every eye turns up - probe the patient - let's bring him home - the one to speak - partisan bickering.

General Nieh was right and I was wrong. He said that a model hospital wouldn't be feasible and I told him I disagreed. So he gave me the people to build it and I went ahead.

When I wanted to build a model hospital, I told Comrade Mao so. I told him I would pay for it with money from home. I told him I would train the needed medical personnel.

Comrade Mao and I talked of many things. I could say that we talked all night. I could say that we only talked for a brief while.

A light shone on the peak of a mountain.
A peasant watched it as it glowed.
One day, he divided all that he had into lots.
He packed only what he needed and started to climb.

Turning down a salary. Turning down better living-quarters than the others. Turning down better food than the rest of the group. Turning down the principle-ship of the school. I need to be free to rush to the Front when a battle is on. I have a cook, a personal servant, my own house, a captured Japanese horse and a saddle. I have no money and do not need it. I have my clothing and my food and nothing to buy. I am not here to be served, but to serve. Fine-tuning the model hospital. Creating an ideal society. An organization like a globe. Round and fluid, moving and dynamic. No bottom and no top. Held together like a drop of water. The cohesion and cooperation of every part. Instruction, supervision, planning. Communication, teaching, correction, modification. Work, and work and work. Training every volunteer to be a leader.

"Delegates to the Chinese patriotic conference elected a democratic government, made up of representatives of all factions in the country. It is to be hoped, the delegates say, that from now on the Chinese can present a unified and effective military response to the invasion of their homeland by the Japanese."

One dollar a month allowance; millet and carrots.
Reading by candlelight; sleeping in a cave.

A person with a terrible pain inside his skull.
An operation on a patient without anaesthetics.
A wolf gobbling lambs, chickens and pigs.

He is lying still in the moonlight. The others are fast asleep. *A weed-devil in the earth.* He lies on a blanket. The grass is wet. He pulls another blanket up across his chest. *A picture of a great green field. One vast farm. One big fertile acre of earth.* His head is against his jacket. It is bunched against a stone wall. The moonlight shines on the valley far below. *A great field overrun with weeds. Choking out the life of the young green corn.* His eyes are as wide as saucers. He looks at the moonlight overhead. Why can't I sleep after such an exhausting day?

Gauze, cotton, crystals of potassium permanganate.
Lack of transport and organization.
Patients slowly dying of sepsis or starvation.

He is a man who dreams on behalf of others.

He brings gifts for which his fellows have not thought to pray.

Comfort for the body - faces covered in blood - the pressure inside the skull - painting a mural - burnt lungs and splintered bones - what I want it to be - the issues of life - a cloud formed over his countenance - a shattered vase - people squabbling among themselves.

Jean Ewen told me that I shouldn't be so demanding of the medical personnel. "You'll catch more flies with honey," was what she often said. I told her that it's the only way to make sure that the standards are high.

Impatience has been my bugbear since the day I was born. Sometimes I have been quite harsh with my personal aide. At times I've been overly-gruff with Ho Tzu-hsin.

There will be gatherings after the workday. Lanterns will shine on contented faces. There will be singing far into the night.

In the beginning, I made a world, said God.
I made it with the calipers in my hand.
I made mankind in my image, after my likeness.
Everything I made, I made of chaos;
There is chaos in everything I made.

My report to Comrade Mao. The model hospital is in place and is working smoothly. It is an ideal organization. A teaching and learning hospital. A training facility for medical personnel. The ripples will be enormous. You will feel the effects very soon. Training every volunteer to be a doctor. Every patient saved is a soldier. We need doctors more than we need food or guns.

He takes a wooden paddle and stirs the dye.

Japanese soldiers posing for photographs.
A god sending a messenger to act as his eyes.
A man who has a mind which is on fire.

Behind him, on wooden racks, drip swathes of cloth.

Galen sewing the bleeding arm of a gladiator. Studying the human body in all its intricacies. Scratching with a stylus as he learns.

The stone walls flicker in the light from the oil lamp.

Have your best thoughts been finally realized?
Would you say you have reached your ideal?

How many doctors do you expect to be able to train?

Gathering around a fire, late in the evening. Shadows on the wall. Candles here and there among the crowd. Pale stars, cold air, silent and thoughtful. Everyone tired and everyone calm at the end of the day. Someone calls out for a song. A little girl – a nurse in training – sets her candle down and stands amid the group. We are an oppressed nation. We must resist our oppressors. Only by fighting can we continue to exist. My interpreter whispers the words. I applaud with the others. Now it seems to be my turn. I sing a song that we used to sing in Spain. No pasaran, no pasaran, no pasaran. More a chant than a song. Spanish words, Canadian accent, Chinese ears. Tired and happy; happy and tired. Content because I am doing what I want to do. Why shouldn't I be happy? I am needed desperately here. No wish and no desire is unfulfilled. I am treated as a comrade. Five-thirty in the morning until nine or ten at night. Under the blanket to sleep the sleep of the tired and fulfilled. Then up again and a day of saving lives. The fire crackles as three hundred sing a song.

Chapter 13

China 3

The sun coming in over the mountain-tops. The valley below the deserted Buddhist temple. Slanting rays on cement roofs. The faint odour of burning
wood. A blackened, brick-strewn compound. Fifty-two miles from the enemy.
The burp of machine guns and the crash of artillery. They could come back in
less than an hour. An old man raking among the burnt ruins. A few boys playing
with scattered bricks. Blackened walls and roofless beams. A flock of pigeons in
an aerial ballet. Very quiet, very still, desolated. I sift among the ruins, but find
very little. Whatever couldn't be taken has been burned.

The sabre-toothed tiger had aspirations.

Peasants making mattresses filled with straw.
A man who schools himself to learn from his mistakes.
A child who is too sick to be let out to play.

The pterodactyl had a gleam in its eye.

An Iroquois healer notes a stand of birch trees. The twigs, the bark the
roots are used to heal. Gout, rheumatism, arthritis, infected wounds.

These same forces are at work in the world today.

Do you ever think of your parents?
Are there siblings somewhere in your past?
Do the Chinese peasants know that you had a wife?

I should have listened to advice. General Nieh knew what would happen and he told me so. But I insisted on having my way. I built the model hospital and now it is gone. Operating theatre, sanitation department, playing-fields. Everything at which I smiled as I dreamed. Cookhouse, games room, lecture hall, medical school, sterilizing plant, drying oven, laundry, incinerator, operating room, drug and gauze room, doctors' office, temperature charts and records. Three weeks it thrived and prospered. The finest hospital in the Eighth Army. Now destroyed by the Japanese. Not one stone left on a stone. They fired all the buildings and took the supplies. I should have known that the Chinese knew more about warfare than I. Humility is a bitter dish for me.

"The Japanese strategy, in the invasion of the mainland of China, has been to mass their armies in frontal attacks against major concentrations of population and resources."

"Experience praises the most happy as the one who made the most people happy."

You wax your skis; you buckle them on; you check your gear. You approach the edge of the slope and take the plunge.

He is about to crack an egg. He is a lad of seventeen. Short and slender and very frightened. He was taken to a cave. Then an inner cave where the doctor was reading a book by candle-light. It was the doctor that I had seen among the troops. The doctor is very gruff. I have heard him barking at others. He stands toe to toe with the commanders and gives them orders. Their faces are grim sometimes, but they do what the doctor says. The doctor looked me in the eye; he didn't smile. He cracked an egg and spilled the contents into a pan. He held it over the fire and the two of us watched it fry. "Aha," he said, and slid it onto a plate. There is a book with many pictures of Canada, where the doctor comes from. I stood and looked at it while the doctor turned the pages. The interpreter says that the doctor says that if I learn to cook his egg the way he likes it, he will give me the book.

Surrounded – north, east, west and south.
Impassible country for all but walking or a mule.

Wounded lying on the cold ground with no coverlets or blankets.

"Bethune is a man who can never accept another's advice. The model hospital was a thrust in his duel with General Nieh."

"Bethune has suffered a major setback. The model hospital was a tentative sketch of his inner-self."

The notes of an old happy song - a wrinkled dollar - the current economic down-turn - the whole idea is so simple - bombers circling lazily - babble in many tongues - the end of the world - a story to tell - a puddle of blood on a stretcher - the battle for the soul.

"We have drawn and used over ninety gallons of blood. I have given over seven hundred blood-transfusions. Be assured that I will soon return to Spain."

To return to being a doctor in Canada again? What would be the point? I had spent too many years taking part in a sham.

The Japanese invasion of the Chinese mainland. The brutal march on the city of Beijing. Chinese squabbling among themselves in a civil war.

Young Proffit glared at the remaining worker.
From now on, you will do his job as well as your own!
And if I ever catch you talking to yourself, I will fire you on the spot!

On the move across the countryside. Inspecting the regional hospitals. A small town cupped in the hills. A treeless horizon and ancient walls. Wounded soldiers hobbling about the streets. Banners and posters on the walls. The war in China; the news of the world. Drawings, poems, criticism, comments. Students strolling along the streets in the faded blue cotton uniforms of the army. Mule-drivers, shopkeepers, messenger boys. On the playground, the shouts of a bayonet drill. Mass singing from a classroom window. The sun shines down from a cloudless sky. Wondering how best to serve. Work to be done; war to be fought; a country to be saved.

"While this strategy has given the Japanese control over many of the major cities of China, and the railway lines that connect them, the Chinese partisans, by organizing the local peasantry, have denied the Japanese control of the resources of the vast Chinese countryside."

Working eighteen hours a day.
Refusing to sleep until ordered to do so.

Medicinal herbs in a garden of Buddhist monks.

A leader bombing factories, cities and towns.
A girl who is distracted by an ancient story.

He stands on a crag and looks along the valley through his binoculars. Painted black so they won't glint in the sun. Waiting for night so we can travel. This is a big country. The mountains stretch away on either side. You can look down one valley and see sunshine on the clouds. You can look down another valley and see the dark clouds of rain. The enemy will never conquer China. The country is too big, the people are too many, the feeling against the enemy is too intense. The enemy wants peace badly. We want a long and protracted war. China is building an army of twenty million men. Binoculars back in the case. Sipping rice tea, kicking a soccer ball, spreading wet laundry on the rocks. Behind him, his troops relax in the sun.

The need to organize medical teams.
Death due to lack of trained surgeons.
Eight thousand men, women and children dead in Nanking.

He is a man for whom no procedure remains unexamined.
He is a man for whom life is a sacred trust.

A cruel and indifferent sky - up out of the mud - giving away my clothing - to think it over - a far-flung thorn - how beautiful the body - eyes are fixed and wary - the scent of heather - a life of drama - a man whom the angels know.

What it comes down to is whether you can live with other people's suffering. Whether you can live among the voices of people in pain. Whether you can turn your back when they call to you for help.

It's simply a case of feeling others' pain. It's a case of feeling others' loss. Every life on earth is precious and must be saved.

There are those who can hear the voices of the suffering. There are those who can hear them no matter where they are in the world. For whom the pain of others is the pain inside their own skull.

The Four Horsemen talked, over drinks, in a tavern.
Outside the window, their four horses munched their oats.
We have been foolish to attack one another.
Let us sign a non-aggression pact.
We need a common enemy to infect, stab, starve, and cut down.
Let us turn our united forces against humankind.

Visiting regional hospitals. Operating constantly. Ten soldiers brought in on mules. Five of them marked for death. Doing the best I can. A shortage of surgical instruments. Knives, artery forceps, surgical scissors, catgut, silk ligatures. Bandages, cotton, gauze, antiseptics, anaesthetics. We need everything we can get. Where is the money I was promised? No word from Canada or the States. My letters seem to disappear. Have they forgotten what the war in China means?

A city. Skyscrapers seen from above. People like black ants on the street. Bats attacking me.

The surprise on Frances's face. At the street corner, early in the morning. Surprising her as she walks to catch the streetcar.

What went wrong for you in Detroit?
What went wrong in Montreal?
What went wrong in Barcelona and Madrid?

Riding on the back of a truck. A hundred miles north of Yan'an. Heading for the Front. Rivers to ford, mountainous roads, open seams of coal. A stream of donkeys with large sacks on their backs. Heading for the hospital at Yen Chuan. Thinking of some valuable lessons learned. The smell of the burning model hospital still in my nostrils. So much for impractical schemes. Stopping at all the small towns. Daily lectures to the doctors and the nurses. Clean-up squads. Fly control. Metal identification disks for patients. Patient files. A recreation park for the walking wounded. Posted duties for all members of the staff. Daily rounds for doctors. Supervising the work of the nurses. The tires dip down in a rut and I sway back and forth. What to do? What to do? Seared deeply by the loss of the model school.

"The Chinese strategy – as devised by Comrade Mao and carried out by such as General Nieh – is to avoid the strengths and to exploit the weaknesses of the Japanese."

"Communism is not love. Communism is a hammer which we use to crush the enemy."

Two people attempting to achieve a meeting of minds.
A knight in shining armour with a long bright sword.
A soldier posting a poem on a wall.

A mud hut on a hillside. The crack of sunrise. Time to load the supplies onto the mules. The doctor opens the lid of a wooden box. I'll have to write another letter home. What is the China Aid Council doing for China? We have exhausted the supply of elastic bandages. I have exactly twenty-seven tubes of catgut left. I have two pounds of carbolic acid. Are you sending more doctors or technicians? Am I to have more medical supplies? I have one knife and six artery forceps. All the rest I have distributed. Five months without any word is a long time. I have two and a half pounds of chloroform. After that is distributed, we will operate without anaesthetics.

One hundred and fifteen operations in a month.
Soldiers standing in pits of water for days.
One hundred and ten operations in twenty-five days.

"Dr. Bethune is always criticizing. He does not understand the realities of the Chinese situation."

"Dr. Bethune is always very angry. At times, he throws his medical instruments around."

The sun, the wind and the rain - the force that moves the heart - the use of plants and herbs - swirling down the drain - no attention at all - the way to cook an egg - a battle of inches - binding up the wounds - a tricycle in a shop - the fundamental strength.

I've often wondered why General Nieh didn't suggest that Comrade Mao turn down my plans. Or why Comrade Mao didn't turn them down on his own. What did those two know that I didn't know?

When I thought of the idea of the mobile hospital, I told Comrade Mao of my plans. It would set up near the Front on the eve of a pending battle. It would save the lives of soldiers who could be swiftly returned to fight in the Front lines.

Many Chinese have mentioned my talk with Comrade Mao. Many have heard that we were alone. Many have heard that we met in a cave.

I have decided what I will do, said the third man.
I will staunch the flow of blood and bind his wounds.
I will take him on my donkey to an inn.
I will leave some money there to ensure his care.
I will enquire of him each time I travel this road.

Pam Tang, a hospital to the north of Chang Chien. Arriving with our gear on thirteen mules. Preparing an operating room. Not far from enemy lines. One hundred seventy-five patients. Thirty-five of them seriously wounded. Lying naked on straw-covered beds. In old and unwashed uniforms. Cleaning and scrubbing two rooms for operation and recovery rooms. A lack of cotton cloth, pails and gauzes. Making do with what we have. Making mattresses of cotton filled with straw. Only enough cotton to make ten mattresses. Sheets, towels, gauze squares, mops, masks, glove cases, all cut out of cotton remnants, sewn and then sterilized. Dividing the patients into classes. Class One – immediate operation. Class Two – danger of infection. Class Three – when there is time. Training the nursing staff. Stressing the need for after-care. Limited experience; limited equipment. Lamenting the loss of so many patients. Feeling that touring and improving hospitals is not enough. Feeling the need to work at the Front. We never see the soldiers who need us most.

"The key elements of the Chinese strategy include wearing the Japanese down with a protracted war, waging guerrilla war in the countryside, and continuing to build a united front among all of the various factions which in the past have undermined the effectiveness of the Chinese resistance to Japanese Imperialism."

Hellishly hot and muggy; rain for two months.
Travelling three thousand miles, four hundred on foot.

A group of people sleeping in a cave.
Healers toiling in a garden.
People eating sandwiches on a train.

Sleep? What is sleep? He no longer knows. He turns, he turns again, he wakes up in a sweat. *Cheaper to steal than to exchange; easier to butcher than to buy.* I lie here – eyes wide open – and I think. *The secret of this war; the secret of all wars. Profit, business, profit, blood money.* The distance from fear to justice is enormous. *Brothers in blood; companions in crime.* The height from what-is to what-should-be is so very extreme. *The beast in them awakens with a snarl.* Like climbing a mountain or walking around the world.

A mule with a broken leg on the side of a road.
Wounded evacuated in the dead of night.
Work, study, sleep, eat and sing.

He is a man who stares death full in the face.
A man who determines that death will be first to blink.

The living of life - a long trip home - the human club - a breath of fresh air - a person washing his hands - the rest of the world - a little red purse - herbs, acupuncture and massage - the wolf is getting bigger - to sleep in the street.

I told Jean Ewen that she needn't bother to come along to the meeting with Comrade Mao. She got on her high horse and insisted she come along. There was so much to discuss that Comrade Mao and I talked until the early morning hours.

Ho Tzu-hsin and I in a tangle of mis-matching languages. How to achieve a meeting of minds? How does one indicate "over-easy" who does not speak Chinese?

The healer will make his contribution. No sufferer will ever be turned away. Disease as a crippling presence will come to an end.

A voice spoke to the doctor in a dream.
Physician, heal thyself! the voice demanded.
Oh, now I see what you mean, the doctor said.
However, it is an extremely difficult procedure.
Am I to assume that you can afford the extra fee?

My report to Comrade Mao. I have had a bitter lesson to learn. I apologize for the loss of the model hospital. I take full responsibility. I am schooling myself to learn from my mistake. I should have listened to your commanders. Every element in this war must be mobile. I am proposing another idea. I have designed a mobile field hospital which can be carried to a battle zone on three mules. There would be three mounted doctors, an operating-room nurse, a cook, two orderlies and two grooms on foot. I will pay for the whole operation with money from home.

What has caused this illness?

A group of people squabbling among themselves.
A wooden box which contains almost nothing.
A person surprising another at a busy street corner.

Should not such a child be let out to play?

Buddhist monks harvesting medicinal herbs in a garden. Sandal Wood, Satavari, Tulsi, Pippermint. Aloe, Turmeric, Pepper, Dalchini.

Why such a look of distress on the woman's face?

How far is Spain from Canada?
How far is China from Spain?
Is China as far away from home as can be?

My plan for a mobile operating team. I will equip them and train them and take them to the Front. Personnel – Dr. Bethune, surgeon, a Chinese doctor, an assistant surgeon, a nurse, an operating-room nurse, a post-operative nurse, a quartermaster, a secretary, four assistants, three grooms for horses and a cook. Equipment – the fifty-bed mobile hospital which was sent here from Geneva.

Cost – one thousand, two hundred and fifty dollars monthly, at no cost to the Chinese. To be entirely borne by the American and Canadian China committees. This will save the lives of countless wounded men.

Chapter 14

China 4

Organizing and educating. Travelling in the mountains. Travelling on the plains. Rough donkey paths along the sides of mountain rivers. Mountain passes of several thousand feet. Down the sides of steep valleys. Walking most of the way. Horses are sometimes slower than walking. Wearing cotton slippers. Wearing them to frazzles. Changing them every few days. Averaging twenty-five miles a day. Dirty, lousy, flee-bitten. Villages scattered along the streams. Sleeping in peasant's houses. Operating in hovels. Mud and brick and stone. Cold and draughty, paper windows, mud floors. Teaching hygiene, anatomy, physiology, medicine and surgery. Everyone very eager to learn. There is oh so much to do. I get very angry with slip-shod medicine. Curbing as much as I can, my own irritability.

A man knelt down on the road from Jericho.

A tourniquet left on for several days.
A pair of scales which weigh an unseen element.
A speaker giving a closed-fist salute.

He raised up another and gave him a drink.

A Neanderthal grandfather telling his grandson all about herbs. Honey, Willow, Mint, Pomegranate. For burns, toothache, stomach-ache and worms.

I offer my services on the road from Jericho now.

Is Communism not a belief like all of the others?
Does it not contain the seeds of the human flaw?
Will brothers not turn on brothers within their own tent?

Visiting the encampments all along the Front and talking with the military commanders. Operating on the wounded and finding unsanitary conditions. Doctor Yang, Doctor Ye, Comrade Tang and myself. Operating on seven wounded in Ho Chien Tsun and Chu Hui Tze. Twenty cases in Hsia Shih Fan. Twenty-seven wounded in Chuan Lin Kiou. Thirty-five wounded at Lia Yuan. They have been on the road for three days without attention. Operating all night and the following day. Admonishing the military commander that neglect of this kind cannot be tolerated! A commander's first duty is to keep his troops alive!

"There has been a change of fortunes in China, in the epic struggle between the invading Japanese Imperial forces and the resisting armies of the retreating Chinese."

"The history of all previous societies has been the history of class struggles."

A pair of skis and an inch of snow. That's all you need. That's how I got started way back when. Pretty soon you'll find yourself racing down the slopes.

He is a wounded Japanese soldier. Not much more than a boy. Captured in battle. His battered arm in a sling. Willing to die for his country but not quite sure how to do it. Watching the doctor operate. Waiting for his turn. Chinese patients, Chinese guards, a Caucasian doctor. There are other Japanese prisoners. Why are they operating on Japanese? His eyes are fixed and wary. Across the valley, peasants bend as they hoe the fields. Somewhere in the north and west of China. A young boy who is a long, long way from home.

A Communism that is simple and profound.
Wounded soldiers dragging themselves back from the Front.
An endless string of deserted villages and fields.

"Bethune is an India-rubber ball. He is either plunging into an abyss or bouncing back."

"Bethune never sleeps. He is afraid to encounter the ghost of his former wife."

Chaos in everything - the mud and the blood - the light of fear - respite for the soul - walking in the woods - the loftiest of mountains - remove these cataracts - must have a purpose - to assign fault - a catalogue of the sufferings.

Asked why I gave the closed-fist salute during my speeches. Explaining, for the umpteenth time, that the closed-fist salute isn't necessarily Communist, but is common to all anti-Fascists. Feeling that I was betraying my deepest self as I said these words.

What to do with a washed-up doctor? Where to hang my shingle out? "A little comfort for the body; a little respite for the soul."

Leave a child to suffer from poverty. Leave an old person to starve to death. You are leaving your child or your parents to suffer the same.

The messenger dared to ask.
If I don't find even one, will it be the end of the world?
The great god rubbed his forehead and thought for a while.
I'll have to think it over while you are gone.

Visiting the military commanders all along the Front and persuading them that our mobile unit should be placed immediately behind the regiments in action, to render operative first aid. Insisting that rest stations be placed on the road from the Front to the rear in order to avoid cases of gangrene from tourniquets left on for several days without attention.

"It turns out that the Chinese strategy has been to let the Japanese believe that they are in control of a territory, when all they actually have are the resources of the capital city."

Feeding my own rations to the patients.
Donating my own blood for transfusions.

Two people miming the way to cook an egg.
Doctors operating all night and the following day.
A man planning to take a long trip home.

Six o'clock. Dark outside. A recess from a conference. Candles lit and placed on the table. The light shines brightly on broad, brown faces. Shadows waver on the wall as they bend and eat. Great steaming pots of cabbage soup. A merry, noisy meal. Rare pieces of pork in a sea of floating cabbage. The difficulties of lifting meat with a pair of chopsticks. Shouts of laughter at the slips between bowl and mouth. Hot steamed rolls made from unleavened wheat-flour. A welcome break from the meeting before they go back to work. Outside the open door, pale stars, cold air, a silent town.

Oil, cigarettes, meat and vegetables.
Japanese bombers attacking hospitals.
Wounded soldiers hobbling about the streets.

He is a man who accounts for every drop of blood.
A man for whom each man's agony is his own.

Your jagged edges - running away from himself - a god rubbing his temples - a vat of dye - a man who schools himself - forming an alliance - every drop of blood - a bowl of cold rice - diagrams of the terrain - an x-ray of all he encounters.

It was simple human logic. People were dying for lack of blood. A source of blood was needed on the battlefield.

In Spain, I saved Germans and Italians. In China, I saved Japanese. I served humanity through Communism; I served Communism through humanity.

The Communists seemed to be bearing the brunt. They alone seemed clean and pure. The 8th Route Army is where I wanted to be.

The troops all saluted the leader and shouted in reply.
We will murder women and children.
We will do this for the cause.
It is essential that all of them should die.
We will follow you into the mouth of hell.

Arriving at Hei-ssu, in the north-west. Checking with the commander of our first aid station. We will be backing up the 8th Regiment, the 7th Regiment and the 9th Regiment, all of whom will be seeing action on the Kuan Lin-lin Chu road. Doctor Wang, Doctor Yu, Doctor Chia and myself and Comrade Tung. Setting up almost equidistant between the three fronts. Collapsible operating table, full set of surgical instruments, anaesthetics, antiseptics, twenty-five wooden leg and arm splints with ten iron Thomas leg and arm splints, sterile gauze and all the rest. All carried here, to the battle-zone, on three mules. Organizing the stretcher-bearers and giving them instructions. This whole enterprise will be an innovation. I expect to see all the wounded who would normally die.

The knight rides on forever. Through desert, mountain and plain, over sand and rock and grassland, he rides his steed through the sun, the wind and the rain. And under his chain-mail coat – next to his beating heart – the torn and perfumed fragment of a kerchief.

Frances and I in our dreams. Me in a burnt-out building and Frances who-knows-where. Dreaming of each other as we turn in our sleep.

Is medicine as old as bows and arrows?
Is it as old as the human club?
Is medicine keeping pace with the tank and the plane?

The battle of Hei-ssu. Working without rest and operating for forty hours. Seventy-one cases who might otherwise have died. A perforation to the lung with hemorrhage who would have had to wait for ten hours before he could be evacuated. A soldier with a skull wound who refuses to retreat to the rear. A patient who dies – a perforation to the intestines – from shock. Doctor Wang giving five hundred ccs of his own blood at three AM in the morning and going on working for twelve more hours. Comrade Tung, with severe tonsillitis and running a high fever, giving over fifty anaesthetics. Doctors Yu and Chia operating on the wounded around the clock. Stretcher bearers slipping and sliding in the mud and the blood.

"Until now, the invading Japanese armies have been moving west and south, assuming that the Chinese are retreating before them in terror at the superior organization, discipline, equipment and determination of the invincible Japanese."

"When we die for the people it is a worthy death."

A young man jumping a ditch.
A contest to see who has the better brain.
A Neanderthal grandfather teaching the value of herbs.

He sits at a small table with a candle and a flashlight. He dips his pen in a bowl of ink and writes on a page. The wall of a ruined Buddhist temple acts as his windbreak. He is planning a trip home, to Canada, early next year. Hoping to raise a guaranteed one thousand dollars a month for his work here. *The China Aid Council, which sent me here, is rather neglectful.* Five hundred miles, on foot, over to Ya'nan. By bus, down through French Indochina. *I have received only three letters from them in over twenty months. The last letter I received was seven months ago.* Then a boat to Hong Kong, and a freighter to Honolulu, avoiding Japan. Then another boat to San Francisco. *They have left me completely in the dark.* Three or four months in Canada, fundraising, and then my return. They need me here. This is my region. I must come back.

Two books on surgery and medicine.
Soldiers existing for days on a bowl of cold rice.
Bandages soaked in dried blood and caked with sand.

"Dr. Bethune is doing what he has always wanted to do. He is helping the sick, the wounded, the dying and the ill."

"Dr. Bethune is dedicated to the service of all humankind. He has compassion for suffering humanity in abundance."

Silent pairs of eyes - we all scramble for cover - the blood will be delivered - a sure-fire scheme - as if the bats are my ideas - people crying, people moaning - not one stone left on a stone - from face to face - onto the rocks - simple human logic.

I went to General Nieh and I told him so. I said, "You were right and I was wrong. I built the model hospital too close to enemy lines."

When the model hospital was over-run, I sent a note to Comrade Mao. I told him that I should have listened to General Nieh. I also told him of my plan for a mobile hospital.

I never talk about my meeting with Comrade Mao. It was private then and is private now. One of those talks that is lit by the glow of one's whole life.

Everyone looked from face to face.
Mothers, fathers, the young and the old.
All we have left in our village is people, someone said.

An infant in a uniform. A lad of seventeen. Shot through the belly. Chloroform. Ready? Gas rushes out of the open peritoneal cavity. Odour of faeces. Pink coils of distended intestine. Four perforations. Close them. Purse strong suture. Sponge out the pelvis. Tube. Three tubes. Hard to close. Keep him warm. How? Dip those bricks into hot water. Bring in another one! Is he alive? He is? Then bring him in! Gangrene creeping in. Forty hours without rest. Seventy-one operations. The battle of Hei-ssu.

"It seems that the tables have now been turned. The Chinese strategy is now coming clear. Now that the Japanese supply-lines have been stretched to almost breaking and the Japanese army has been thinned, the Chinese have struck a damaging blow from the rear. This is the first great Chinese victory of the war."

Examining twelve-hundred wounded; performing over seven hundred operations.

Rising at six in the morning and working all day.

A hospital on the backs of three mules.
A belief containing the seeds of the human flaw.
A messenger contemplating the end of the world.

He is in a field near a village on the side of a mountain. The members of the mobile field hospital are asleep. Three mules – tethered to stakes – graze nearby. *A criminal war of aggression; mass murder; authorized madness.* I have had no sleep tonight. Too much to think about after a day of having no time to think at all. *Chinese partisans; Japanese troops. Brothers in poverty; companions in misery.* What are the thoughts that come between us? What are the words that will close our wounds? *Lying wounded, side by side. Looking up at the stars and thinking of home.* Must be almost morning. Resting my head on a bandage-bag. Love to have the peace of mind of a grazing mule.

A hoe, a mattock, a mule, a wooden plough.
The need for food and cod-liver oil.
The singing of ancient songs with new words.

He is a man who leaves no gemstone unexamined.
A man who was born with a pair of x-ray eyes.

Murder women and children - an inventory of the world - three children lying dead - the young, green corn - ninety gallons of blood - the warm water on my legs - agony and disease - the seeds of the human flaw - an endless rain of bombs - this cannot go on.

Interesting to think that I couldn't seem to get along with people. And it's people who will remember me after I am gone. Jean Ewen will certainly want to get in a word or two.

Me saying "over-easy" and "sunny side up" in English. Ho Tzu-hsin saying whatever he was saying in Chinese. Both of us miming the perfect way to cook an egg.

The health of the mind. The health of the body. The health of the spirit.

I shall keep these scales forever; I shall never throw them away.
They remind me of the things that I wish to weigh.

My report to Comrade Mao. One third of all cases escaped without infection. Still more need to cut down on the time between the wound being received and the time of the operation. Need more dressings at the rest-stations. This would cut down on infections for sure. All fractures were operated on at once and splints applied. None with fractures of the skull have died to date. We now work close to the scene of the action. We now see all who would have died.

We have demonstrated to our own satisfaction, and I hope to the satisfaction of the Army commanders, the value of this type of treatment of wounds. It is expected that it will revolutionize our present concepts of the duties of the medical service. The time is past and gone in which doctors will wait for patients to come to them. Doctors must go to the wounded and the earlier the better.

What is the cause of this washing?

A doctor hanging out a shingle.
A man whose skills seem blessed by the gods.
A person giving another person a drink.

Ignorance? Poverty? War?

The healing power of Maori medicine. Makomako, Mamaku, Manuka, Titoki. A gum to chew, a poultice to soothe, a vapour to inhale.

Why does she slap the cloth with such a bleak look on her face?

Can you picture yourself at Mycenae?
Can you picture yourself at Troy?
Were you not a doctor in the trenches in 1915?

Somewhere in China, near Hei-ssu. Late at night in a clearing in an orchard. A kerosene lamp on a tree. A great circle of soldiers and medical volunteers. Singing together the ancient songs of their country. New words giving voice to their current concerns. Serious, optimistic, clear-eyed and serene. They know that victory will come if they will only endure. The mobile field hospital has been a great success. I lean back and listen to the singing. The voices carry on the breeze. I have no bitterness in me. I work eighteen hours a day. I'm having a swell time.

Chapter 15

China 5

Midnight. Cold and clear. Stars in the sky as the sparks fly up from our fire. A rider comes out of the shadows. Comrade Mao will see you now. I will take you to where he is working. Our leader often works far into the night. A narrow trail to a small village nearby. On a dark street at a small house, we stop.

My teeth and eyes are bad; completely deaf in one ear; a chronic cough.

A leader saluting his troops.
A dyer stirring cloth in a vat.
A physician who claims that he has no crystal ball.

I am as far away from home as an arctic explorer.

A string of camels swaying along the Route of the Silk. Information passing up and down. The healing powers of herbs, acupuncture and prayer.

Madrid has fallen; I am in China now.

Do you see yourself as god-like?

Do you bring people back from the dead?
What does Jesus mean by Physician heal thyself?

A man stands facing the door. Blue cotton army uniform. On the table, a cotton cap with a red star. From a distance he would look like any other soldier. High forehead. Thick black hair. A beaming smile. Thank you for coming to see me. You are welcome at any time. I hold out my credentials. A letter from the Communist Party of Canada. Not necessary. I know quite well who you are. He gestures towards the chairs and we both sit down.

"One thing has become clear about the protracted war between the various factions which are fighting for the soul of China. Undoubtedly the man who is emerging as holding the future of China in his capable hands is a man named Mao Tse-tung."

"Revolutions are the locomotives of history."

Not everybody skis back home in Canada. There's a lot more going on than just ice and snow. Sometimes I dream that everyone gets to ski.

He settles his back against a rock and catches his breath. Boys of twelve; old, old men. Rifles, swords and spears. Two hours of climbing to get to this spot. "The Japanese will never suspect that we are here." He clenches his fist on the spear. Some of the older ones have guns. Hiding here in the dark and waiting for word. "A Japanese patrol is heading this way." Forty partisans have attacked a patrol of a hundred Japanese. They killed six of the enemy and then they melted away. The Japanese troops will soon be below us. Now it is our turn to kill. I will be brave when the word is given. I will rise up and throw my spear. They will be trapped like fish in a pool. This is the way we will defeat the Japanese.

Grain in woven bins and earthenware pots.
A soldier with a piece of a bomb in his back.
People for whom Communism is a way of life.

"Dr. Bethune is the kind of man who yells at people with a devilish gleam in his eye. He challenges other people as much as he challenges himself."
"Dr. Bethune is a person whose heart is right. There is a calmness of spirit that is gradually descending upon him."

Future healers of the wound - taking part in a sham - ancient songs with new words - the fragment that had been missing - studying the human body - a spoon in his hand - we fall all over the place - sand, rock and grassland - to dwell in the valley below.

Being asked, for the umpteenth time, whether I am a Communist. A reporter for the *Winnipeg Free Press*. Blurting out that yes, of course, I am a Communist and proud to be so.

No shortage of agony in the world. Turn on the radio; read the news. All you have to do is look around.

If you could hear a voice from half-way across the world. If that voice was crying in pain. What would you do?

Superior eyes, ears, nose thinks the dog.
Superior mind in a crisis, thinks the man.
The man and dog walk deeper into the woods.

The candle shines on the table as we talk.

"Your spirit, your utter devotion to others without any thought of self is shown in your great sense of responsibility in your work and your great warm-heartedness towards all comrades and the people. Every comrade must learn from you."

"In a series of brilliant essays, Mao has laid out a strategy which might well decide the future of the people who are struggling for a fair share of the benefits of life on this earth."

Trudging along snow-covered trails.
Racing to battles on horseback.

Two comrades sitting at a table.
A light shining on the peak of a mountain.
A man who is swatting pesky flies.

Two young girls sitting side-by-side at a meeting. One of them raises a hand and they whisper together, uncertain as to which of them will be the one to speak. The two are dressed like the chairman of the meeting. Faded blue jackets and trousers. No ornaments of any kind. Broad sunburnt faces, thick black hair, cut short and bobbed. The chairman recognizes their right to speak. One girl stands up and looks down at the other. The other one stands up and takes hold of the first girl's arm and the first one turns and begins to speak. She tells the assembled delegates that the evacuation work near the government offices was done successfully, where it was supervised, but not so well at the places which were further removed. The delegates listen intently. The second girl nods in agreement and holds her partner's arm as the first girl speaks.

One trained physician for thirteen million people.

The need for clothing, socks and gloves.
A wild, bare, hot and treeless country.

He is a man who knows no heroes and no villains.
He raises everyone up to stand beside himself.

Holding a broken child - what might go wrong - exhaustion and despair
- distracted by an ancient story - treated as a comrade - old as bows and arrows
- perched on the rocks - a distant beacon - bleeding to death on the battlefield - a
pair of x-ray eyes.

I took the simple human need. I took the advances in storing blood. I put
them together and made a mobile blood-transfusion service.

It was simply a case of logic. If the wounded can't come to the hospital,
the hospital must come to the wounded. I put a hospital on three mules and set
out for the Front.

The Canadian-American Medical Unit. Dr. Charles Parsons, an American Surgeon; Jean Ewen, a Canadian nurse; and Dr. Norman Bethune. Leaving
Vancouver, on the Empress of India, to sail for Hong Kong.

I cannot see into the future, said the physician.
My instruments do not include a crystal ball.
The dove and the scorpion have an equal claim to life.

His elbows are on a map of the Chinese landscape.

"No one who has been at the Front has failed to express admiration for
you whenever your name has been mentioned, and none remains unmoved by
your spirit."

Staggering in the desert. Two lovely female forms on a high cloud. Beck-
oning me to cross. Thin and weak with a staff in my hand. Staggering across the
plain. The scattered wrecks of covered wagons.

Frances and I, each living close, a few blocks from each other, in Montreal. Meeting in a neutral café – the best of friends. Idle chatter about how happy
we have both come to be.

Does one dominate people for their own good?
Does one liberate people for their own good?
Does one dominate them in order to liberate them?
What does an analysis of history tend to show?

His secretary brings us rice tea.

"No soldier or civilian is unmoved who has been treated by you or has seen how you work. Every comrade must learn this true Communist spirit from you."

"Comrade Mao has encouraged the Chinese to cast aside two very powerful beliefs: that Japan will win the war and that the war will be over soon. He has stressed that the war will be a long one, that the sacrifices will be great, and that China, if it is true to itself, will eventually be victorious against the Japanese."

"We shall heal our wounds, collect our dead and continue fighting."

A man who can hear a voice from across the world.
A person dreaming that everyone gets to ski.
An angel dressed in long white flowing robes.

As deep a sleep as he has enjoyed for a long, long time. *How beautiful is the body; how perfect in its parts.* Where am I at this time? In my apartment in Montreal? Sleeping in the mobile-unit by the roadside, somewhere in Spain? Tossing and turning on my cot somewhere in China? *It moves with such precision: obedient, proud and strong.* I am in all these places at once. Shells explode; rifles crack. A bloody soldier lies on the table in my tent. *How terrible when torn. The flame of life sinks lower and lower and threatens to flicker out.* Resisting the blackest dreams. Bringing a child back to life as I lie here sleeping. Oblivion, like a blanket, keeps out the chill. Another long night of saving the bruised and the torn.

A peaceful and prosperous republic of workers.
A line of mules snaking along a river road.
The technique of doing a dressing or sweeping a floor.

"Dr. Bethune doesn't sleep very well. When General Nieh ordered Dr. Bethune to sleep, due to exhaustion, Dr. Bethune got very angry with General Nieh."
"Dr. Bethune is as fresh as a daisy in the morning. By late afternoon, he seems to have aged at least twenty years."

Through another person's eyes - the hands on the tiller - the better brain - hunting for coals - the way life is - an inhuman wall - the fire crackles - other people's suffering - devoid of vanity or ambition - the perfect way to cook an egg.

I told General Nieh exactly what I had learned from the whole experience. He was gracious enough not to say that he'd told me so. That is, if my interpreter conveyed the General's actual words.

When the mobile hospital was a success, I sent a note to Comrade Mao. I said that the mobile hospital is a success and will save many lives. I was always open and honest with Comrade Mao.

Most of the time, Comrade Mao and I talked of practical things. The need for doctors, nurses, supplies. The most important thoughts we read in each others' eyes.

A light shone on the peak of a mountain.
A peasant climbed to the top.
When he got there, he found a star.
He opened up his pack and started to work.
He built a dwelling there and lived in the glow of the star.

The two of us sitting and talking.

"Your spirit inspires everyone. We must all learn the spirit of absolute selflessness from you. With this spirit, everyone can be very useful to the people."

"Should China win its war against the invading Japanese, there is no doubt that Mao Tse-tung will emerge as a towering figure in China, and – given the population and the size of the emerging nation – a major figure in future events on the world stage."

Operating in a derelict Buddhist temple.
Sleeping only six hours a night.

A man and a dog out walking in the woods.
An arctic explorer moving across the tundra.
A man who holds a scalpel in his hand.

Six o'clock in the morning. Extremely cold in this room. He moves over and opens the door to the outside world. *I am the only person alive in the world.* Over the distant, faint-blue mountains, a pale line of light in the East. *Everyone who has ever lived; everyone who is now alive; everyone who will ever live in the future.* In an hour, the sun will be up. *I am all the people in the world; all the people in the world are – simply – me.* Boil some water and make some tea. No use going back to bed. Too many thoughts racing around inside my noggin. I can never go back to sleep. Once my eyes are open, that's always it for me.

Women, men and children carrying bedding and pots and pans.
The need for gauze and bandages and absorbent cotton.
The burning of villages and the raping of women.

He is a man who looks quite through a man's reputation.
He holds all men whom he encounters to equal account.

A person absorbing another person - exactly what I wanted to do - seared deeply by the loss - the blessing and the curse - things that I wish to weigh - the value of herbs - the words of a healer - a group of people talking - a painting or a vase - the ills of all humankind.

I didn't have time to molly-coddle. Too many things that I wanted to do. Jean Ewen's grandchildren will be better off because of me.

Not too runny and not too dry. After a number of frustrating attempts, Ho Tzu-hsin learned to cook my breakfast the way I like it. There is a photograph of the two of us together, with Ho Tzu-hsin holding a book and me enjoying Ho Tzu-hsin's first perfect egg.

Mankind is capable of living an ideal. Ours to realize; ours to deny. I pledge to work towards this end until I die.

I made a world for mankind to live in, said God.
I made it with the calipers in my hand.
I gave dominion over every living thing.
Everything I made, I made of chaos;
There is chaos in everything I made.
But I don't feel guilty, or cruel or indifferent.
There is a scalpel within reach of every hand.

His eyes bore into mine.
"A man's ability may be great or small, but if he has this spirit, he is already noble-minded and pure, a man of moral integrity and above vulgar interests, a man who is of value to the people."

Why is he working so late at night?

A man with bad eyes and a chronic cough.
A person holding the future in his hands.
A peasant watching a glow from a distant mountain.

Why the grim look in his eyes?

The Inuit healer boils the snow and stirs the pot. Berries, herbs, lemming skin, seal fat. Treatment for the soul, the body, the mind.

With what colours is he dying the swathes of cloth?

Does Mao catch flies with honey?
Or does he swat them with Marx's book?
What will be left when all of the pesky flies are gone?

The secretary enters the room again and waits. Comrade Mao rises and walks over to him and listens to whispered words. The whispers cease and the secretary turns and leaves. I rise and stand by the table. You must excuse me. Pressing news. I am called away. We bow to each other. We shake each other's hand. He turns in one direction and I turn in another. Outside the house, my horse is held as I swing up onto the saddle. As I ride, the air is cold and very clear.

Chapter 16

China 6

Operating under fire. Operating while a partisan brigade is under attack. A young boy with a leg fracture. Have him patched up in no time at all. Just a boy, but I would love to make him into a doctor. Making doctors out of peasants. Boys and girls from one-story mud and stone houses, from villages in the mountains, who have never been in a hospital before. Working quickly before this boy loses any more blood.

I am the only person.

A girl with ruddy cheeks and an apple complexion.
A man painting a mural inside a cage.
A physician riding along in a jaunty roadster.

I am the only person alive.

A sick daughter sweating feverishly in the tent. Hunter-gatherers searching in a meadow. An elderly woman finds the precious herb.

I am the only person alive in the world.

How do you track the path of a life?
How do you mark the rises and falls?
How do you measure what has been done and what has not?

Operating with an infected finger. Impossible to avoid. Operating without gloves in these dirty wounds. A strapping big soldier this time. Must be about eighteen. Had to persuade him to let me amputate his leg. Hopelessly smashed by a bullet. He absolutely refused. Without it, he would never be able to fight the Japanese. I promised an artificial leg and a job with the general. If he'd kept the leg, he would have died. We all meet bumps in the road. Better an infected finger than losing a leg or a life.

"The China Aid Council has announced that it has lost track of Dr. Norman Bethune, the prominent Montreal society doctor who did so much to raise awareness of the world-wide fight against Fascism. When last heard from, he was organizing a medical unit in support of the Communist 8th Army in Northern China."

"Love thy neighbour as thyself."

The powdery snow. The beckoning slopes. There was a time when all I wanted to do was to ski.

Neighbourhood children painting pictures. A dozen or so some week-end afternoons. Spread around the apartment floor. Cans of paint and horse-hair brushes. Every colour of the rainbow from which to choose. The adults standing around and talking. Looking out the window as the snow falls on the street. Some of the cars struggling to cope with the ice and the snow. The children making art-work of their present hopes and fears. The adults whispering their fears of the future – pouring more whisky into the glass – and wondering what in the world they can possibly do.

The enemy as fish in a pool.
Meals of noodle soup, pork, eggs and tea.
An organization like a drop of water – like a globe.

"Comrade Bethune is the most valorous fighter on the Front of the emancipation of mankind. His internationalist spirit is worthy to be learned and respected by all Chinese people."
"Comrade Bethune, with his great love, his sympathy, his courage in struggle, achieves the highest standard of revolutionary virtue."

An infected finger - granted none of the liberties - a set of scales on his mantle - torn and perfumed fragment - a tiny crust of bread - an arctic explorer - hunted animals - other tides, other oceans - to achieve a meeting of minds - overrun with choking weeds.

Doctor Archibald and I, at the Victoria Hospital, locking horns.

Marion, in my apartment, inviting the children to savour the cans of coloured paint.

The nuns, at the Sacré Cour, doing everything they can to help the poor.

It was Young Proffit's first day on the job.
He was the son of the President of the Conglomerate.
He was now Vice-president of Everything That His Father Owned.

Uncontrolled chills and fever all day. Fainted while operating and had to lie down. Temperature hovering at 39.6 degrees. Jouncing along on a stretcher, over mountain trails. Leaving Shih Chia Chuag Hospital of Central Hopei Troops and travelling north. Physician, cure thyself! You are the one who is charged with knowing! You are the one who swings into action when sepsis sets in!

"After his speaking tour of North America, on behalf of the Republican Movement in Spain, Dr. Norman Bethune took a party to China in order to fight what he called the Fascist scourge, by which he meant the Japanese armies who had invaded that land. He told friends that he intended to set up a medical service which would be in support of the Communist 8th Army, somewhere in northern China."

Riding on a litter in the mountains.
Thinking of skiing again, when the war has finally been won.

Two people melting together.
The fragments of a shattered vase.
An eagle perched on a nest.

He is riding down from Paris, with Sorensen at the wheel, jotting ideas down with a pencil, a clip-board on his knee. Once in a while, hitting a pot-hole and cringing as medical instruments clink and clank in the back of the truck. Making plans for something the world has never seen. A bag of buns with some slices of ham and a flask of local wine. A small bridge with a creek and a grove of trees. "And if the refrigerator fails," he says, "we can cool the blood in the creeks," as he reaches for his pencil in the grass. "Just think about it, Sorensen. It will be a whole new way of saving lives."

The partisan as a worker in uniform.
Constant dust, cold air and piercing wind.
A hundred wounded men on a railway line.

He is a breath of fresh air in the medical profession.
He is the man who is setting medicine on its ear.

A stunning mountain view - all that you have - back from the dead - only healed scars - an extremely difficult procedure - rehearsing your final words - the negative and the positive - the value of herbs - continue to rain death - race with the clock.

The Spanish doctors, in Barcelona, giving blood transfusions to those who arrive from the Front.

Sorensen, Sise and May, the Blood Brothers from Canada, driving all over Spain, with clinking milk bottles filled to the brim with donated blood.

The soldiers of the Ski Patrol, in the Guadarammas, who were kind enough to lend me a pair of skis.

Pestilence sat alone with his drink in a tavern.
Outside the window, his white horse munched his oats.
I have tried to infect War but to no avail.
I need a less-formidable foe to destroy.

Being sent back from the Front against my objections. Protesting that my work here is not yet done. Insisting that I be kept informed of any abdominal cases of fractured femur or skull cases. Insisting that the doctor is never sick. All I need is a bit of rest! No one else knows better than I! I have felt fatigued before and have carried on!

An Angel. Kindly & benign. She is holding a baby. Beautiful & bright. A small churchyard with tombstones.

To be able to walk down any street in the world. To be able to look any-one in the eye. To be able to say: I allowed you to be you; I was always me.

A girl. Apple cheeks. Ruddy complexion. The scent of heather in her hair. The girl and her young man arm in arm. A freshet chuckles cheerfully through the glen.

Was it Frances or was it me? Impossible – not even desirable – to assign fault. Not for nobility – but for accuracy – I accept all blame.

Do you think in terms of self-evaluation?
Is there anyone who would be qualified to evaluate you?
What is the measuring-stick that such a person might use?

Vomiting all day with a high fever. Being carried on a stretcher through the mountains. Reached Tu Ping with a small band of soldiers. Carried west to join the 3rd Regimental Sanitary Service east of Yin Fang. The infection is spreading beyond my finger. Fear of gangrene. The regimental commander has ordered me sent back into the mountains. Useless for work.

"The whereabouts of Dr. Norman Bethune continues to be a mystery. Neither Dr. McClure nor Nurse Jean Ewen, two Canadians who have worked with Dr. Bethune in China, has heard from him for many months. They say that they suspect that the dispatches and letters which Dr. Bethune undoubtedly would have sent must have disappeared amid the chaos of war-time China, while en route to Canada and the USA."

"On a blank sheet of paper, free from any mark, the freshest and most beautiful characters can be written; the freshest and most beautiful pictures can be painted."

A girl with the scent of heather in her hair.
A man painting a picture late at night.
A horse munching oats outside a tavern.

They meet in a room in a cave, and they talk for most of the night. He tells the leader of his plans to build a model hospital for the training of medical personnel. Of his wish to develop a mobile operating-unit which could follow the shifting front and operate on the wounded as the battle rages, saving hundreds and thousands of lives to fight for the cause. At every sentence of translation, the leader nods. They talk far into the night. They both have practical plans. Each forgets, as their ideas ebb and flow, to take an occasional sip at his cup of rice tea.

A doctor with the heart of a lion and the hand of a lady.
Air raid warnings as Japanese bombers fly overhead.
An end to poverty, ignorance and feudalism.

"Comrade Bethune's sacrifice is celebrated by our fighting men and leaders. Our courage is multiplied a hundred-fold by his example."
"Comrade Bethune is regarded by the Chinese nation with love and admiration. Someday all progressive mankind will cherish his memory."

A cup turned upside down - holding an x-ray up to the light - the glow of one's whole life - mission aborted; credit denied - suckling a child - the centre of the world - a meeting place for ideas - the locomotives of history - a tangle of mis-matching languages - a numbed face.

Jean Ewen, alongside the mule train, binding up the wounds from the bomber raid.

Comrade Mao, in our meeting, acknowledging the value of my work.

Ho Tzu-hsin, in the morning, somewhere in the hills, beaming with pride at the perfection of our morning egg.

Three men met at an inn.
They were tired and they were dusty.
The servant had already washed their feet.

Vomiting on the stretcher all day. High fever, over forty degrees. Either septicaemia from the gangrenous fever or typhus fever. Writing a letter to Lang Lin, my interpreter. Dictating in English to an old fellow who walks beside the litter as we walk. Many years ago he was a schoolboy in Hong Kong. We need more money, more materials, more medical personnel. Send this letter to my colleagues in Canada. When I get well, I must return home. I must return to America and Canada and tell the people about the needs of the people of this region. We need more of everything they can send for our medical work.

"Letters and telegrams to Dr. Norman Bethune have gone unanswered. No one in Canada seems to have any knowledge of where he is now or what he is doing in China. The China Aid Council is appealing for information from anyone who can help. There is aid sitting in warehouses in Canada and the United States which awaits further word as to where to send it."

Being carried on a stretcher in 1915.
Thinking of ways to save as many lives as I can.

A man on his first day on a job.
Two love-birds dancing to the sound of a gramophone.
A scroll with an inventory of the world.

He leans back, exhausted, with his head against the cushion. Her head – Frances's head – is on his shoulder, and he can see their reflection in the glass. On a rack at the end of the railway car, a stand of a few dozen skis. Small groups play cards or quietly talk of the day and how it's been. The pulling of wine bottles out of canvas sacks and sandwiches from paper bags. And all along the railcar, couples sleep. The girls with their heads on their lovers' shoulders, sleeping the sleep of the tired and fulfilled. A perfect day on the slopes. Perfect weather, bracing air, perfect snow. Frances sighs as if she is dreaming. He leans his head against the cushion and closes his eyes.

Implementing a five-week plan.
Hard-boiled eggs, wheat rolls and steamed buns.
A people with a common aim.

He is the doctor with a heart of gold.
His compassion for his fellows knows no bounds.

Gods of ourselves - a series of problems - no shortage of agony - strug-
gle back into life again - to dive all the way down - a cat on the train - a wall
of books - good and fine and free - more alive than other people - pain over my
heart.

Frances, lovely Frances, amid the heather and the mist, deciding whether to jump the ditch or not.

A voice spoke to the doctor in a dream.
Physician, heal thyself! the voice said.
Oh, I can do that, the doctor replied.
I shall increase the size of my waiting room.

Riding on a litter, somewhere in the hills. Blotting out the pain by tightly squeezing my eyes. Dreaming of coffee, of rare roast beef, of apple pie and ice cream. Of mirages of heavenly food. Dreaming that books are still being written; dreaming that music is still being played. Dreaming of dancing, drinking beer and looking at pictures. Dreaming of clean white sheets in soft beds. Dreaming of women who love and are willing, in turn, to be loved.

A mud hut on the edge of a village. A carpenter planes a piece of wood. Another stops to chat and they whisper their words.

The ebb and flow of the seasons.
The sun's eye watching us all day.
The cycle of the days and months and years.

A rocky gorge at the edge of a village. The water tumbles and gurgles down. As clear and clean as the snow that melts in the hills.

A Roman doctor visiting a villa. Checking a man whose eyes are blind.

You will see when I remove these cataracts.

Darkness in the village. The moon is not visible in the sky. The stars shine, but not enough to light the way.

What is the inventory of light and darkness in the world?
Have you altered that balance by even one iota?
Would you say that yours has been a valid life?

Can't seem to sleep at night. Mentally very bright. Phenacitin and aspirin, woven's powder, antipyrine and caffeine all equally useless. Dr. Ch'en arrived this morning. If my stomach settles down, I'll be fit to travel. Very rough road over mountain passes. The doctor is giving a consultation. Asking me to give him the symptoms. Always the doctor; seldom the patient. At the other end of the scalpel this time around. I lie here on my litter. Cool breeze, blue sky, sunlit snow. One of those beautiful days in the mountains. Skiers attack the slopes early on days like this. Feeling slightly better today. Steady pulse. Clear vision. A sharp and persistent pain above my heart. I'll just close my eyes for a moment and get some rest. Then I'll be up and on the go in no time at all.

Three Books

Bethune: The Only Person Alive in the World – a novel
A young Canadian doctor, Norman Bethune, sets up a practice which he hopes will lead to money and prestige; however, his social conscience leads him on a journey through the Canada of the Great Depression, the Spain of the Spanish Civil War, and the China of the Chinese Civil War and the Japanese invasion. Ultimately, the journey becomes a quest to understand the world in which he has found himself living, to develop a compassionate response to that world, and to discover the essence of himself as a human being.

The Making of The Only Person Alive in the World – a reflective journal
This journal records the author's reflections on the process of the crafting of the novel as it evolved through the stages of planning, writing, editing and polishing. It constitutes an effort to be as conscious as possible of the process whereby the single idea that suggested the topic of the novel was expanded into a complex work of art. Topics range from the nuts and bolts of novel-building to the nature of the novel as an art-form.

Planning The Only Person Alive in the World – a planning notebook
During the writing of the novel, the author kept a hand-written notebook which records the day-by-day development of the novel as it found its shape and style. The notebook – now in print form – reveals how a vast cluster of thoughts was sifted, selected, structured and polished into novel-form.

The Project
Together, this novel, journal and notebook comprise the eighteenth installment in an on-going novel-writing project in which the author is exploring the concept of form and meaning in the novel, and of the novel as a form of expression in the twenty-first century. All of the published journals and notebooks are available for free download at www. johnpassfield.ca.

About the Author

John Passfield was born in St. Thomas, Ontario, Canada, and continues to reside in Southern Ontario, near Cayuga, with his family. He has taught and studied literature, creative writing and drama, and is interested in the development of the novel as an art-form.

Novels by John Passfield

Grave Song
The Agony of Robert Chisholm

Jumbo
P. T. Barnum's Greatest Creation

Pinafore Park
The Swan Boat Incident

Water Lane
The Pilgrimage of Christopher Marlowe

Rain of Fire
The Ordeal of Conductor Spettigue

Victoria Day
The Fabric of the Community

The Wright Brothers
Flight is Possible

Leni Riefenstahl
The Valley of the Shadow

Babe Ruth
Out of the Park

Raskolnikov
Murder with an Axe

Sergei Eisenstein
Death Day

Albert Einstein
Wondrous Strange

Geoffrey Chaucer
Canterbury Bound

Ospringe
A Visit with Grandad

Pompeii
Vesuvius Dominus

Beethoven
The Ninth Immersion

Job
The Cornerstone of the Universe

Bethune
The Only Person Alive in the World

Terry Fox
Somewhere the Hurting Must Stop

Lord and Lady Macbeth
Full of Scorpions Is My Mind

Visit www.johnpassfield.ca for more information.

In Search of Form and Meaning:
Journals by John Passfield

Each journal is a day-by-day record of the complex process that a writer undergoes while crafting a work of art. It records the largest decisions, of structure and theme, and the smallest decisions, such as the choice of one word over another, and the constant interaction between the two. Each journal is a record of a writer's reflection on the craft of novel-writing.

The Making of Grave Song

The Making of Jumbo

The Making of Pinafore Park

The Making of Water Lane

The Making of Rain of Fire

The Making of Victoria Day

The Making of Flight is Possible

The Making of The Valley of the Shadow

The Making of Out of the Park

The Making of Murder with an Axe

The Making of Death Day

The Making of Wondrous Strange

The Making of Canterbury Bound

The Making of Ospringe

The Making of Vesuvius Dominus

The Making of The Ninth Immersion

The Making of The Cornerstone of the Universe

The Making of The Only Person Alive in the World

The Making of Somewhere the Hurting Must Stop

The Making of Full of Scorpions Is My Mind

Visit www.johnpassfield.ca for more information.

The Novel as an Art-Form: Planning Notebooks by John Passfield

Each planning notebook is a printed version of the hand-written notebook which records the planning, writing, editing and polishing of each novel. Each notebook is an attempt to record, understand, and organize the vast cluster of thoughts which occur as one grapples with the various levels of organization which a clear yet complex work of art demands.

Planning Grave Song

Planning Jumbo

Planning Pinafore Park

Planning Water Lane

Planning Rain of Fire

Planning Victoria Day

Planning Flight is Possible

Planning The Valley of the Shadow

Planning Out of the Park

Planning Murder with an Axe

Planning Death Day

Planning Wondrous Strange

Planning Canterbury Bound

Planning Ospringe

Planning Vesuvius Dominus

Planning The Ninth Immersion

Planning The Cornerstone of the Universe

Planning The Only Person Alive in the World

Planning Somewhere the Hurting Must Stop

Planning Full of Scorpions Is My Mind

Visit www.johnpassfield.ca for more information.